The
Starfish People

The Starfish People

Leann Marshall

Copyright © 2007 by Leann Marshall.

Library of Congress Control Number:		2007906200
ISBN:	Hardcover	978-1-4257-6871-3
	Softcover	978-1-4257-6861-4

All rights reserved. No part of this book may be reproduced or transmitted in any form or by any means, electronic or mechanical, including photocopying, recording, or by any information storage and retrieval system, without permission in writing from the copyright owner.

This is a work of fiction. Names, characters, places and incidents either are the product of the author's imagination or are used fictitiously, and any resemblance to any actual persons, living or dead, events, or locales is entirely coincidental.

This book was printed in the United States of America.

To order additional copies of this book, contact:
Xlibris Corporation
1-888-795-4274
www.Xlibris.com
Orders@Xlibris.com

To my baby sisters, Amy and Abby

Love is Forever

"Our humanity were a poor thing
Were it not for the
Divinity
Which stirs within us."

—Bacon

1

Tuesday, May 4, 2202

3:35 a.m.

The nightmare comes on as if it was only waiting for my eyes to close. It always begins the same way: light glinting in bright starbursts on churning water all around me, the slap-slap sound like the liquid punctuation of water moving against me, against a harder surface—a boat? So much water and light that it blinds me to anything else that might be there; if there is something or someone else there, I can't see for all the glare and the waves that pump up and down everywhere. And me, with nothing to grab onto, thrashing my arms and legs to stay above water but inhaling air tinged with salt into my lungs, gasping—*Is this my last breath before I go under?* Leg muscles burning and arms punching through water and air, hands clawing for something, anything that can pull me up, pull me out, give me a chance—*Help me help me help me* . . .

I cannot fight anymore my legs and arms are so heavy if I could I would cry out but I'm holding the last breath with my lungs they are burning already I could not pull in enough air that last time the water rose around me so fast or did I just go under I feel so heavy so heavy the light is gone I think murky I actually think of the word murky and in the darkness I see pinpoints of light in my eyes like tiny flashes I am going down and down and I struggle to look up but I'm not sure where up is anymore my brain is playing tricks no air my lungs are burning my eyes feel too big for their sockets my chest begins to heave on its own I cannot think I cannot see I cannot understand why and the only thing I finally see is a face above looking down at me through the murk a white shape with two dark places for eyes I cannot see who it is and it moves because the water moves but it sees me and it knows and it does not help me it does not help me . . .

My chest expands on its own I cannot help it the cold water rushes into my lungs but there is no relief—*No air! Cold water pushes everything out pushes from the inside out my lungs are ice they heave they cannot push the water out help me God oh God help me help me help me . . .*

And then the dream ends as it always does—I spiral feet-first down into darkness before I wake so breathless and so drenched in sweat, I almost believe I have really drowned. I struggle to sit up in my bed, the sopping sheets twisted like a cold, sucking eddy all around me. My racing heart skips a beat. I think I have been holding my breath the whole time.

10:45 a.m.

There is an ancient clock in Dr. Moore's office that marks time with long, dreamy passes of its heavy pendulum. For several long seconds its soft, measured *tock* is the only sound in her yellow and blue office, as I stare at this woman across from me that I thought I knew well. But this . . . it isn't like her to deviate from her usual conservative perspective on things.

"I don't understand. You're saying I drowned." I search her face for any sign that will betray an odd attempt at a joke, but I see nothing. Now it's my turn to smile. "Maybe we need to switch seats. I'm still here. I'm not dead."

Dr. Moore leans forward, startling me. "Think of what you just said," she says.

I frown. "I'm not dead?"

"No, before that."

Still frowning, I mentally rewind. I'd told her I couldn't do this anymore, that nothing has made any difference—not the systematic desensitization stuff or the progressive therapies or anything else we've tried over the years. The dreams are still there. The fear is still there. It's always been there, and it's not going away. I shake my head, look at her.

"What you feel like near water," she prompts.

"I've told you and told you," I say, my voice lifting in frustration. "When I get near a pool of water bigger than that fountain outside, I feel as though I'm dying all over again. And I don't know why."

She's nodding, and now she slaps the ever-present notebook arranged neatly on her lap in triumph. "There! You said it again: 'I'm dying all over *again*.'" She opens the notebook and flips quickly through its pages. "Here." She follows along with her finger. "September 26, 2196: 'I am fighting to stay above the water but I know it's no use.' And here—February 19, 2198: 'I feel the water closing in around me and look up to see if the face is there above me like before.'" She flips more pages. "July 8, 2200: 'I'm so heavy and tired and I'm sinking, and I remember how dark it is, how murky.'" She looks up at me. "You are always referring to what happens in this dream as though you already know what's going to happen."

I almost laugh, although I don't find it funny. Is this some off-the-wall tactic of hers? "Obviously, I do know what's going to happen. I've had this dream jillions of times." I feel the familiar twisting in my stomach. Just talking about the dream is unsettling. I remember my promise to myself: this will be the last time I come here.

Dr. Moore closes the book and her mouth twists into what I think is almost a smile. "How long have you been having this dream? As far back as you can remember, is what you have said. I'll say it again: What if this dream isn't a dream at all, but a memory? What if this really happened to you?"

Dr. Moore lays the notebook on the small table beside her chair, carefully sets her pen beside it, and turns to me. "Many years ago, psychiatrists put patients into asylums when they didn't know what else to do with them. Many of those patients were actually very normal. Oh, they had problems, all right—chemical imbalances, instability resulting from some sort of trauma, all kinds of things we now easily recognize and treat with wonderful results. But now more than ever, we do realize how complex the human mind really is, and that we don't and may never know everything there is to know about it. And sometimes, even now, we still don't know what to do in a particular case. At least we know better than to assume it's hopeless. We don't just throw people away if they don't fit within the parameters of what everyone considers normal."

Well. At long last, I know that I'm not normal. Now I've hit bottom.

Dr. Moore's blue eyes hold my own dark ones as though she's reading my thoughts. "I'm saying this isn't hopeless, Sera. I wasn't sure before, but now I think it's time to approach this fear of yours with something rather unorthodox; something I will explain, if you would like to hear about it. Then, when you've heard me out, you can take some time to decide, because there are some risks. Don't take too long, though—you only have until tomorrow morning before the peak opportunity for you will pass, and it isn't likely to ever come around again."

My mouth becomes dry as I listen to Dr. Moore explaining this last-ditch therapy. She hasn't used those words, of course, but that is what it is. My body is tense although my hands remain relaxed, palms up in my lap. I want her to believe I'm calm. Although I remain skeptical, I find my firm resolution to give up therapy giving over to curiosity. She's explaining something I have read a little about, but of which I have no real knowledge. I am not a techie, by any stretch.

"You know about the recent strides in practical Kinetic Regression Travel?" she asks me.

I nod, licking dry lips. "I read the news."

"Good. Then you have at least heard of Dr. Shipley's institute. Dr. Shipley was a colleague of my father's, back in the day. They were among the original group of scientists who developed the KR Transport Vehicle which, along with EyeCom, has been revised more than a few times for practical time regression and retrieval." Dr. Moore seems excited, but speaks slowly and deliberately. "It involves sending a subject back to a particular, predetermined point in time to observe and even encounter the being that housed that individual's energy in a previous life."

There's a long silence in the room with cheerful, country blue furniture and polished wood floors as I try to absorb what Dr. Moore is saying. I know that her father was involved in the initial experiments. I know that her father has been retired and out of the limelight for many years due to a deteriorating brain illness for which there is no cure. I know that Dr. Moore feels her father's peers slighted him when he was not included in the Nobel Prize, for whatever reason. None of this is a secret—in fact, it's widely known. Dr. Moore has a great personal interest in the transport vehicle.

I know that the first experiments with human regression travel ended badly, grotesquely devastating the surviving traveler physically and mentally, and although the problems were eventually identified and corrected, the margin of error still remains, and there is still risk. Anyone who occasionally grabs a copy of *The Global Mark* at the corner newsstand knows these things.

Dr. Moore shifts in her chair. "It has already been shown that such an experience can have a positive impact as part of therapy. Life-changing, in fact."

My hands are no longer resting palm up; they seem to be clutching the arms of my chair by their own volition. "I don't understand. You're saying that I should risk being rearranged into some kind of mutant for a jaunt back in time to drop in on one of my old selves, so I can somehow quit having nightmares about drowning. Well, isn't that passing the buck a bit? And how in hell can I expect my past self to fix me when I can't even fix myself in the present?" I blink stupidly, unable to comprehend my own sentence.

Dr. Moore, as usual, remains composed after one of my sarcastic flare-ups. She is amazingly patient with me, I know. I also know that I tend to lash out whenever I'm totally confused, as I am now. Stubbornness is one of the negative qualities I must have inherited. I force my rebellious hands back into an anxious little heap on my lap and relax my neck and shoulders. I really must get more sleep.

"All very good questions, Sera," Dr. Moore says. "I can certainly understand if you have misgivings about all this, but I can assure you I would never even suggest it if I thought you would be in any kind of real danger. You would be prepared down to the smallest detail; Dr. Weiss—who worked as an assistant to Dr. Shipley for years—and I would oversee everything. There could be intermittent communication between us, you would have some crucial foreknowledge about your former entity, and it would be as safe as traveling on the Line you took to get here."

She continues before I can work up another lather. "We each have a unique energy signature that remains constant and unchanging. When the body that temporarily houses it no longer exists, the energy, although altered, continues to move forward in time, to and through different physical vehicles. You already know how EyeCom can find anyone anywhere, anytime, by scanning his or her unique energy signature."

I nod. EyeCom is biometrics at its best—or worst, depending on your current state of affairs. If you're a snot-nosed toddler separated from Aunt Trixie at the MegaMall, EyeCom can zero in on you in a snap. If you're an escaped prisoner on the lam, you can expect EyeCom to rat you out, and have you back in the slammer before you can blink twice. This morning I placed my hand upon the scanpost before boarding the Blue Line, but even that isn't necessary anymore. EyeCom keeps track of everything, even the fare you owe to cruise across the city to visit your shrink. I carry no money, no ID and no numbers. I'm my own credit card.

"Well, in this case, EyeCom identifies your past specific physical entity, and keeps track of your own present one when you go through time regression. It's integrated with the KR Transport Vehicle. As long as you're careful to follow the rules, your unique energy signature remains safe and intact at either point in time."

I look at her, still skeptical. "Dr. Moore, that doesn't explain how going back to a past life could help with my phobia."

She nods. "In anticipation that this moment might come someday, Sera, I have already used EyeCom to do the necessary energy sig regressive ID research on you, and to bring up obituaries, records, whatever I could find connected with the entity found. I believe I have located the point in the past where your phobia originated, the point in time when your past entity experienced the original cause of it. This gives us—you—the opportunity to travel back to that time, to observe and understand the original circumstances that ultimately led to your nightmares. And from there, your phobia should be less complex to treat."

"How do you know you have the right person—the right point in time?"

Dr. Moore's blue eyes darken. "The entity has *your* energy signature. The entity drowned, and I can't find any past record that explains how or why."

My eyes are steady on hers. "You said I only have until tomorrow morning to make my decision. Why didn't you tell me sooner?"

She sighs. "I probably should have. In fact, I had planned to let this opportunity pass without telling you. But in light of your father's death, and the fact that you want to discontinue therapy, I think it's the right time, after all. But again, it's your decision."

Light entering the tall window at the end of the room sends muted shadows lengthening across the floor. I sit for a long while, turning all of this over and over in my mind. Although I consider myself a fast learner, the questions that crowd my mind now are so complicated that I cannot see an end to them. Dr. Moore is silent and allows me time to think.

I can't hear the clamor of the city through the thick windows, but I'm aware of it just the same. Outside, people are moving along the streets and sidewalks and railways in steady, unbroken streams, like ants, hurrying to get wherever it is they go, with whatever purpose it is that propels them along. It's unceasing, even when night comes and darkness tries to move in. The lights come on everywhere, allowing constant, never-ending motion forward and forward and forward.

And here I sit in this small office, frozen to my chair, with nowhere to go from here. I have been coming to this place for a long time. Although I dread coming here, in some ways it is the only thing I can rely upon—Dr. Moore is the only one familiar with the dark places I have been. I think of the countless times I have sat here in this chair facing hers.

Earlier this morning, when I arrived for this appointment, there she was as usual: an attractive, mature woman in her late fifties with her silver hair cut short and wavy, today clad in a dark blouse and fitted, light tan skirt.

"Sera, hello." She'd smiled as she settled regally in her blue overstuffed chair and crossed her legs.

I smiled back at her and headed for my usual chair, the one under a particularly lovely landscape depicting an oak tree and a fence. I'd waited for her to set her small spiral notebook in her lap, ready for occasional notes. There was a time I was fascinated with that notebook, sometimes purposely saying something out of the blue like, "Yesterday I saw a woman in the grocery store wearing red and I had an enormous desire to scream," to see if she might lift her pen in her manicured hand and jot down something. But as time went on and we got more involved in the real things, I didn't play little games like that anymore.

She rested her hands on the notebook. "I was so sorry to hear about your father."

"Thank you," I'd said, and waited for and then felt the pang in my heart. Not because I miss him; he was never really there. But because now I am, in all the world, profoundly alone. I have no siblings, no cousins, aunts, uncles, godparents—no one at all to consider as family. My few friends are involved with their own lives. I have no one.

Now I sit considering this, and more. They say I'm wealthy now, but there is no richness in my life. Dark circles surround my tired eyes. Nightmares invade my sleep. I have no energy for a steady social life, and so I have no real friends, only occasional, short-lived reunions with a few people from school. To stay connected with the rest of the world, I hold a job at the coffee shop down the street from my apartment; I can handle nothing more complicated. The nightmare has taken over everything, and beyond all reason. I *am* drowning. I don't have anything to lose.

I already know I am going to do it. Dr. Moore is pleased.

As I take the elevator down to the crowded street, I find I don't feel like being alone. I want to talk to someone who doesn't yet know Father is dead, because I don't want to talk about that. I walk straight to the Talk Bank and grab one of the wires and say "Arie Bastion" into it. Almost immediately, she answers.

"Arie," I say, "this is Sera. I'm just down the street. Meet me for lunch?"

I get to the Thai Room first, and an elderly woman seats me in a booth with my back to a large fish tank. As soon as she leaves I get up and slide into the seat opposite instead. I check out the menu but it's the same as always—algae noodles, algae rice, and spicy kelp noodles. I don't know what it is I expect to find, but whatever it is, they don't have it.

Finally Arie slides into the seat across from me. "How long has it *been*?" She says, without even saying hello.

"I don't know—four, five months? You look great, Arie," I tell her.

She beams, her hair and skin flawless. "All the latest products," she says, pointing to her face. "I was due. I found a *line* on my forehead New Year's morning, I want you to know. I cried all day. Why didn't you tell me I looked like a beast the last time you saw me?"

"Because I thought you looked great then, too."

She smiles. "You're just saying that to make me feel better. Of course, you're lucky. You have that timeless look. Women like you don't age."

I lean back in my seat. "We're only twenty-five, Arie. Give it time. I'll be a beast before you know it."

She stares at her menu and rolls her almond-shaped eyes. "Same old thing." She drops it onto the table and leans forward, chin on palm, straight black hair falling around her hand. "That's when it starts, you know."

"What?"

"Twenty-five. That's when the real aging begins. My aesthetics circle says the sooner you start with the products, the better. It makes surgery totally unnecessary. You could have skin like this well into your nineties."

I smile and shake my head. "So what have you been doing with yourself, Arie?"

"Oh, just doing all those lawyers' dirty work for them. Cele is the worst of the bunch, always wanting me to do her research for her. Worse, she even wants me to shop for her husband's birthday gifts." Her perfect nose wrinkles. "This year he got eel skin underwear. I have a feeling she'll be doing her own shopping next year."

The same woman who seated us comes and takes our order: two spicy kelp noodles.

Arie unfolds her napkin and lays it in her lap. "I am also doing some research on my own."

"About?"

She looks around dramatically and then at me. "Food preparation."

"Food preparation, you said?"

"You remember those history videos in school about back when people prepared their own food—cooked it and everything?"

"Yeah. We thought it was kind of gross."

"Well, this man I'm seeing now, he's into that kind of thing. But so far I've had zero luck finding any books on the subject. How to make the food, that is. I don't know where to start."

I shift in my seat so Arie blocks my view of the fish tank. "Why is it so important to impress this guy?"

She looks hurt for a second. "I don't know. I like him. What about you, Sera? Don't you want a relationship? Isn't that important to you?"

I look at her. She reminds me of Dr. Moore, pestering me with questions. Again I am back in that office, sitting in my chair under the painting after admitting my sadness at being alone.

"And whose fault is that?" Dr. Moore chided gently. She doesn't say things like that often. I hadn't felt like arguing, defending myself. It would take too much energy. I'd already used that up on the journey to her office. Instead, I looked at my shoes.

"Sera, I *am* sorry for your loss. I know you weren't close to your father, that you hadn't seen each other for a few years. But you had to have known this was coming for a long, long time. You have pushed away good opportunities for relationships with those who seem to have genuinely cared about you. You're too young to become a hermit."

I'd rubbed my ear, still staring at my feet. One of my shoes was badly scuffed. I wondered if there was anything I could do about it, short of buying another pair, then decided against that—I'd make them last, wear them scuffed.

"What was that young man's name—Thomas?" Dr. Moore pressed. "You talked so much about him, and the two of you really seemed to enjoy each other's company."

A sigh erupted from my lungs and I rolled my eyes like an adolescent. "Please don't bring him up again."

She'd rested her elbows on the chair arms and laced her fingers together, touching her index finger to her mouth. When she does that I know she's exasperated with me. I'd straightened my spine, her perfect posture again making me aware of my own.

"I've explained how he grew up water skiing and boating and fishing and how he was planning for the two of us to go on a world cruise," I said. "I mean, the man had water instead of blood running through his veins."

"But when you finally told him about your phobia, he was willing to adjust his life around you. He wanted to work it out."

I'd clenched my teeth and fidgeted. My words came out too loud. "I'm not having someone rearrange his whole life because of my fear. I was attracted to him because he was so active and unafraid and—*out there*. You know? We would have eventually resented each other. I know that. I think I considered him more of a friend, anyway."

Dr. Moore rested her hands in her lap again. Waited.

For a moment a strange feeling ran through me—a feeling that something important was about to happen, as if she and I were both balancing on the crest of a wave, unable to see over to the other side. Then I felt an awful pulling along my face, shoulders, and spine, as though a creature clung inside me, trying to claw its way out, but failing. Tears should have come, but the creature had sucked them all up; my eyes remained dry. I felt as though I stood at the bottom of a dark, empty well, and there was no rope. *This must be the bottom.*

Now I look up—Arie is staring at me from across the table. "Sera? I said, don't you want a relationship?"

"For what?" I ask, trying to sound pleasant. "Do you know I've been running around this city all day, and I haven't seen one child?"

Arie plays with her napkin, saying nothing.

"Yesterday I saw a school carrier. I think there were only three children on it. Three."

She looks up at me, her face sad. "That's why we have to concentrate on other things, Sera. Don't you see? Life goes on. *There are other things.*" She looks uncomfortable—no, almost panicked. It's like I've made a wrinkle.

I smile at her and wish I hadn't been so harsh. She's never been the type to look at anything straight on. Especially anything painful. Maybe that's why I wanted to have lunch with her. "I'm sorry, Arie. I haven't been sleeping well lately; my nerves are a little raw. And you know what? I think food preparation is a great idea, really. Call me immediately when you can cook something besides spicy kelp noodles."

She smiles at me and finally laughs.

When our food comes, we talk more about skin products and Arie's new boyfriend and food preparation. I don't mention anything about my father, and she doesn't ask me about Thomas.

* * *

There are things to be done. Distasteful things. Instead of taking the Blue Line, I lease a lightcar and drive forty miles into the country, to my father's house. As I glide along, steel and glass give way to trees and green, rolling fields.

I used to live in the house too, but I never thought of it as my house. I haven't been out this way in five years, not since I swallowed my pride and came to ask Father for help.

I find I can pretend I'm all right until I turn into the fenced drive that winds through a shady arbor to the house. It's then that my hands grip the wheel and I feel the familiar flutter in my chest, even though I know Father is not there.

I lay my damp palm upon the scanpost at the door, and as it opens I step through and stand just inside the great empty foyer, flanked on each side by a towering staircase. A huge chandelier hangs in the center, its hundreds of prisms glittering with daylight shining through the open door. The heady scent of jasmine, my mother's favorite flower, hangs in the air. Father made sure it was always present, all those years, until it has permeated the very walls.

The silence is not quiet. It shouts at me from every corner with raised fist. It is all as overpowering as I remember, and once again I feel very small. I resist a childish urge to sneak up the stairs to my old bedroom. My room, with its dreamy posters and stuffed animals piled on the bright quilt and stacks of my favorite books and magazines and stray socks draped over the chair at my cluttered desk, was my haven. Father never entered my room. The rare times he wanted to talk to me, he stood stiffly outside the door and stated his business in the low, terse voice he always used with me, not noticing the room or its furnishings or the cluttered state of it at all. My room was my world, something he could not and did not want to know. This particular fact didn't bother me as you would think. At least, when I settled in my room at the end of the day, I felt as if I had something of my very own, although it was part of my father's house.

The pull of the stairs is strong. Instead, I direct my feet to walk under the chandelier and through the wide arched doorway, making my way down the long main hall into a darkly paneled room.

I marvel at how nothing has changed. Thick rugs cover the wood floor; a large stone fireplace fills the expanse of one wall, along with built-in bookshelves and brass sconces. Leather upholstered sofas and chairs and side tables are grouped along another, and before the heavily draped windows on a third wall, a solid mahogany desk presides over the room. Taking a shaky breath, I straighten my shoulders and walk to the desk. I begin opening drawers. I don't need a key—Father never kept them locked; he knew I would never dare go through them without permission. The heavy drawers open and close smoothly, solidly.

I can almost see him behind the desk, so intent on whatever he is writing that he doesn't look up when I enter the room. *"Father,"* I say, *"I'm home."*

"I can see that," he says, still writing.

I fidget and wish he would look at me. "I know you wanted me to finish out the year, but I just couldn't handle the—"

Now he looks up, his face flushed with anger. "You just couldn't handle—what? I provided a good education for you, gave you all the opportunity that anyone with half a brain would need to get through business school and make a decent life for herself, be an upstanding, contributing member of the community. I pulled strings for you. And all you had to do was hold up your end of the deal. But you just couldn't handle it, could you?"

I fight back hot tears. I don't want him to see me cry as though I'm a little girl.

"Well, I hope you can handle the fact that I'm disappointed in you, deeply disappointed, Sera."

"But Father, it isn't that I don't appreciate all you've done. I would still like to go to school. Maybe if I did something else. I just don't have what it takes to—"

"That's quite evident. Now, if you'll excuse me, I've got work to do."

I blink and the chair is empty. He isn't here anymore, I remind myself. He can never send me away again.

I hear a footfall behind me.

"Is there something I can get you, Miss?"

I whirl around, my heart leaping wildly, and then have to laugh—even if a bit hysterically—with relief. It's only Mister. He has been a part of this house as far back as I can remember. I can't recall his working name. I began calling the android Mister when I was barely able to talk, because he always called me Miss. He is now archaic, his kind replaced in other households through the years by much more sophisticated models. Father was always slow to change to new technology, unless it was absolutely necessary. And now that Father is gone, Mister is of no use at all, like the furniture that sits unused and gathering dust. Doubtless he was in sleep mode until my movement stirred him back to life. He stands in the doorway, his arms at his sides, his funny, angular head tilted a bit, his shiny eyes focused on me.

I remember when I was a girl, I would lie alone in my bed at night, trembling in the dark after the nightmare. I was too afraid to call for Father, because he would be angry if I awakened him for something so childish. So I would call for Mister in a desperate stage whisper, knowing the android would be able to hear it no matter where he was, and when he appeared at my bedroom door he would say, "Can I get you something, Miss?" And I would say, "I'm afraid, Mister." And he would say, "Were you drowning again, Miss?"

"Yes," I'd say.

Mister would look around the room before saying, "There is no water, Miss. You are quite safe. Will there be anything else?"

"No, Mister."

"Very good, Miss."

And he would leave. What I most needed was someone to hold me, but at least Mister would show up when I wanted him.

Now I'm almost as happy to see him as I would be an old friend, but although he does recognize me, I know Mister cannot perceive the time that has passed since he saw me last. To him I have only been gone a moment.

"Is there something I can do for you, Miss?" he repeats.

"No, Mister, there's nothing, thank you."

"Very good, Miss." He turns and disappears down the hall, heading back to his last post, wherever that may be.

My chest heaves with a sigh, and I turn back to the desk. I stuff papers and anything I think might be important into an old briefcase I find propped against the desk. I know the lawyers already have all the papers of any real significance for the estate that they need, but it's important to me that I can do this.

I'm turning to go when I see the small, simply framed photograph always present on this desk, and I pick it up. A beautiful young couple embraces, smiling happily in each other's arms, seemingly oblivious to the unseen photographer. By their expressions, they are wildly, unashamedly in love, as only ones so young could demonstrate so completely in such a small snapshot. They are like two movie stars to me, beautiful and glamorous, and totally unreachable. I slip it into the briefcase, and walk down the long, still hall and through the foyer, my footsteps echoing on white marble. I step out onto the porch, turn, and close the massive door. I will have the lawyers take care of everything. There is no need to ever come back.

There's one more stop I must make before I can go home. I drive the lightcar back into the city and deposit it in a drop zone at the curb near the Cosmos Coffee Shop. Derek is wiping up a small spill on the counter when I enter. I stand and watch him for a minute, smiling. I've never known anyone who loves to clean and shine things like Derek. The coffee shop may be foundering, but anyone can see it's the cleanest place in the city.

He looks up and smiles, surprised to see me; I have been off for the two weeks since my father's death, trying to get things in order. "My best worker," he says. Then his wide, dark features fall a little. "How was the funeral?"

I don't know how to respond to such a question. "It was a funeral."

Derek nods as though satisfied. "You want coffee? Tea? O2 fix? It's on the house."

I glance over to the Breather, where a woman in a business suit plops down upon a worn sofa, deftly grabs one of the brightly colored hoses snaking from the octopus-like tank, caps it with her personal breathing device, and sucks in a deep swig of oxygen laced with one of many breathable gases. Her shadowed eyes become unfocused and she sways in ecstasy.

I turn back to Derek as she bursts into high, hysterical laughter. "You know I'm trying to quit," I say. Derek smiles. "Anyway, I can't stay. I came to let you know that I'm going out of town for a couple more days. Starting tomorrow."

Derek stops swiping the counter. A deep line forms between his eyebrows. "Come on, now—don't do this to me. I need you tomorrow, Sera. Tondine didn't show up again today, Macy has a weekend class, and Ire called to tell me he's at home in bed with something again. Some*body* is more like it."

I shake my head. "I'm sorry, Derek. You know I wouldn't do this unless it was important."

Derek crosses his muscle-bound arms and glares at me for a moment, then throws his beloved rag down onto the counter, letting the air escape between his teeth. "Damn it, Sera—how long?"

"Just a couple of days, that's all."

"You'll pull double shifts when you get back."

"Absolutely."

He slowly turns his massive back to me, and resumes swabbing. "See ya," he says.

The woman in the business suit smiles at me brightly when I leave, and waves with the hand that isn't holding the hose tightly to her nose.

There is a dull ache behind my eyes by the time I palm the scanpost and enter the lobby of my apartment building, lugging my father's briefcase. It's Friday, and there's an aura of excitement as people hurry home from work and ready themselves for City Fair. Music has already started up in the streets, and soon we will hear and feel the deep humming from the track as the Wheel starts its slow journey around the perimeter of the city. I wish I could feel as charged as everyone else, but I only want to go up to my apartment and take a cool shower, eat something, and go to bed.

A tall, striking man exits one of the elevators as I'm walking toward them, his electric blue eyes and strong, assured stride unmistakable. He's not alone; a young woman scarcely out of her teens bounces beside him, bubbling with excitement. I make a run for the elevator before the doors can close, but it's too late.

"Sera—Sera, *here!*"

I'm frozen by Thomas's rich voice. I was always frozen by his voice. I turn to feign seeing him for the first time. "Thomas! How have you been?"

Thomas lives in my apartment building, but because it's so large, we rarely see one another. Not anymore.

I turn to the girl and smile. She has stopped bouncing, and stands gazing at me. She wears loose, silky pants that ride below her bejeweled navel. They are chromatophoric, and flash frantically with shapes and colors. Instead of a top, she has painted a layer of pink DermGlo over her shoulders and down each breast, as though she wears a glowing, transparent bolero. Her shoulder-length, honey hair is braided, each braid entwined with a green neon Doosa. They're not real, but they twist and squirm like actual snakes, and recoil with the slightest touch. She has painted dark circles around her green eyes, and bright pink, glittery goo covers her pouty lips.

Thomas has played it down, wearing only a white tunic with opalescent DermGlo in his black hair. He answers my question. "Doing okay. I'm sorry I didn't make it to the funeral."

I nod. We both know why he wasn't there. It would have been uncomfortable for him. "It's okay," I tell him.

Thomas appears flushed and well. He seems none the worse from our breakup, and I am ashamed of the stab of disappointment I feel because of it. Then it occurs to me that perhaps he is flushed and happy only because I am here. I feel my own face warming. Why can't I stop this barrage of silly thoughts when I'm around him?

He holds my gaze a moment too long. The girl beside him punches him lightly. "Oh," he says, "this is Neeta. Neeta, Sera."

Neeta shoots him a look, then turns and smiles as she looks me up and down. I smile back. She winds a finger around one of the thrashing emerald Doosas. It grows bright with panic.

"I thought they outlawed those things," I say to her.

"Just the ones that *bite*," she says, still smiling, and links her arm tightly through Thomas's.

He hasn't taken his eyes off me yet. I feel uncomfortable.

"Obviously we are cruising the Wheel tonight," he says, gesturing with a hand at their garb. "It'll be here any minute. Want to join us?" By his tone, Thomas really means it. Neeta shoots him another look, but he doesn't notice. "I bet you haven't been out with your friends for a while. It isn't good to be alone all the time. Join us."

The ache behind my eyes is becoming a dull throb. How dare he assume I never go out? How dare he think that I can't have fun without him? "No, thanks; I can't. I stayed up pretty late last night partying, and I'm wiped."

Thomas smiles. "I understand. Look, maybe I can give you a call soon?"

I think I should tell him I'm taking a trip, but it all seems so complicated, and I don't have the energy to explain. Instead I nod and shrug, still smiling like a fool.

"Okay." He glances at Neeta, who tugs at his arm. She's getting bouncy again. "Well, we're off. Take care."

"You too. Have a good time."

Now I feel the vibrations in the floor, and in spite of myself I hurry to ride the elevator up to my apartment so I can at least watch the arrival. By the time

I unlock the door and set down the briefcase, gulp down an aspirin with a swig from a bottle of water, and slide open the glass balcony doors, I can see it.

Darkness in the city falls mottled and red, never winning out over the tall, windowed buildings that ascend like spires of light against it. Muted music and the racket from the crowds rises from the street far below, through misty air filled with the aroma of hot pretzels and kelp dogs and popcorn. The Wheel approaches on its low platform from the east. It is gargantuan, standing at least fifty stories high, and the main hoop housing its mechanics blacks out the lights from buildings behind it as it rolls to a stop on its great, smooth track. This is the last stop to let on more people; when it resumes, it will not stop again to let its occupants off until early morning.

"*Ripping!*" I say out loud to no one, admiring the thousands of multicolored lights that emanate from the edges of the glass hoop moving slowly inside the main hoop. In spite of my mood I am mesmerized by the Wheel, although I have never ridden it. I lean over the balcony railing, watching the lines of people entering the Wheel from three different levels to disperse within the glass hoop. It takes several minutes for the throng to board. When the Wheel reaches maximum capacity, those still on the street cheer and wave to those inside.

Finally, the Wheel resumes its motion, and the crowd below roars a tremendous send-off. As it moves alongside my building, I can see the people on all the levels inside the glass wheel as it rolls slowly in the opposite direction within the main wheel. People rise from below me, hundreds of them, as though standing inside a huge Ferris wheel with glass floors instead of cars. They come level with my balcony, then descend again down the other side. They are partying, some dancing to the Wheel's own music, which overwhelms that on the street. I recognize "Echo" by Black Frenzy—it is fast and pulsating, like a thunderous heartbeat. I see people crowded together, laughing and shouting to be heard above the din. Others linger at the glass, looking out at the city, at me watching them, drinks in their hands. Most of them wear illuminated clothing and DermGlo, and neon Doosas that make their hair seem to dance with light that casts an eerie glow over their excited faces. Some wear only chromatophoric skins over their own, and they are like walking light shows with flashes of color playing over them. As the Wheel rolls slowly by, I feel the wash of wind from its wake in my face, hear the whooshing grind of its workings. It is like a huge, kaleidoscopic creature pulsating with life, leaving me behind. Somewhere inside, swallowed up by the thundering giant, I think as I watch it move away, are Thomas and Neeta—*together*. And I can't feel anything at all.

Later I sit cross-legged on the floor of the living room, with my back against the sofa. The balcony doors are still open so I can hear the street music, which has slowed down and sounds more like jazz. A light breeze has come up, playing around the open doors. It rustles the papers from the briefcase that I've laid out all over the floor, and they shift a little. I am eating some kind of seafood linguini dish that I nuked, fishing my dinner from the small carton with chopsticks. Thomas taught me how to use them without dropping the food into my lap. It took a while for me to get the hang of it, but he was very patient with me. I would say I am an expert now.

I have singled out the picture frame from the clutter around me. I hold it up so the light glints off its brass sides, and then turn it so the back is toward me. All my life, I have seen this black velvet backing with its fold-out stand upon Father's desk from the hall; sometimes, as a young girl, I would sneak into the study, dark except for the thin light coming in from between the heavy drapes, and tiptoe around behind the intimidating bulk of the massive desk, curiosity outweighing fear. I'd climb up onto my knees in the wide, leathery chair that smelled like pipe smoke, stretching forward with my arms across the desktop so I could finally see the front of the picture frame and the photograph inside it.

Now I flip it over easily in my hand. Once again, I am astonished by the charming, boyish young man in the picture, the way he looks so unlined and animated and happy. I never knew Father to be any of those things. It is easy now to see how I resemble him—the dark eyes and hair, the fair, good skin.

But the image of the young woman beside him fascinates me most—her flawless, cameo face, her lovely, sparkling blue eyes accentuated by the perfect arch of her brows, the fine, straight nose, the line of her full, smiling lips over perfect white teeth, the way her chestnut hair falls in shimmering waves onto the delicate curve of her long neck. I have carefully studied these things about her, and more—the way one exquisite arm is thrown assuredly over Father's strong shoulder, her graceful, feminine hands, the slight tilt of her head that suggests playfulness, perhaps even a hint of mischief. I can almost imagine the care she must have taken with her makeup, hair, and dress, the morning of the day she was photographed with her lover.

I have gleaned all I can from this one flat likeness, because it is all I have of her. If ever there existed another picture or holodisc of her, Father has destroyed them or hidden them away. I have never found any.

I set the photo down on the table beside the sofa, shuffle the mess of papers into a disordered stack, toss the empty food carton into the compressor, and rinse the chopsticks. Although my headache has subsided, I'm beginning to dread sleep, and decide to make a quick list of things that need to be done before tomorrow. I settle on the bed with pen poised over a blank pad, trying to gather productive thoughts, pushing others away.

In the morning I will return to Dr. Moore's office, where I will meet Dr. Weiss on familiar ground. Then we will take a lightcar to the institute, which lies only a few miles outside the city, and the two of them will go over the things I need to know before my journey. Dr. Moore has already explained that my travel experience is only to be an observational encounter, and that, while I am allowed to come into contact with my past entity and family, I cannot impact them with any major change or else I—and others—could be in great peril. She has said that if I can find out what exactly caused the person to drown, it can do more for my self-enlightenment than several more years of office therapy.

Although the thought of all this is unnerving and somewhat creepy, I cannot help the flood of curiosity that wells up inside me: *What will the entity that housed my energy be like? Was I male or female? Did I have children? Was I a good person, or did I deserve to die in such a horrible way? What were the things that were important to me then?* Any answer for the last question would be especially interesting, since I cannot answer it for myself even now.

There is no use in packing any clothes, because Dr. Moore will have to provide them for me. Fabrics and style have, of course, changed since the point in time to which I will travel. The few things I will take with me must be contemporary with the times, with the exception of a small bag that contains a tiny first aid kit and a wristband communicator disguised as a Mickey Mouse watch. Also I will be given the appropriate kind of credits, called money—much more than I will probably need. Actually it is my own money, because I am giving the institute a generous cut of my inheritance. Without her saying as much, I know that Dr. Moore has jumped at this chance—as her father's daughter—to provide funds for this project, to gain the publicity and renown she believes he deserves. I know that this is the primary reason that I, as a civilian, am being allowed to go at all. If I were seeing another therapist I would not be getting this chance. At least I do not allow myself delusions concerning the motives of others. Father has taught me well.

Any nondigital mail I receive in my apartment building while I am gone will automatically be forwarded to my hold box after one day; each daily copy of *The Global Mark* will be sent there, as well—I could get digital copies of it, but like some others, I have always liked to feel the paper in my hands. I have made sure the lawyers are aware of everything. It occurs to me to call Thomas and leave a short, polite message for him, explaining my absence. Again I see his smiling face, Neeta's arm linked through his. I decide not to call after all, and that I might as well go to bed—the only item I have written down is *Sleep*.

As soon as I close my eyes sleep intertwines my restless thoughts with soft, fuzzy gray tendrils and obscures them, but only for awhile. Then I am in the cold water once again, shivering with dread, lungs convulsing for air. When finally I awaken, this time I'm crying. I lie exhausted in my bed, staring into the dark. I have left the balcony doors slightly ajar, and a welcome whiff of air feels cool on my sweaty skin. The streets below have grown silent, the Wheel having made its return stop long ago. It is the stillest time of all in the city, the few hours left before sunrise.

In spite of it all, I manage to get a little sleep during these last hours, and the alarm sounds for awhile before I can rouse myself enough to slap at it. As I trudge by the balcony doors I can see it's gray and raining outside, the sky filled with mist and gloom. I decide to forego my morning run. It is easy to rationalize—I have a longer journey to make today.

I pour steaming coffee from a bottle into a cracked blue mug, and thumb through the *Mark*. Among the slew of articles there are the usual, never-ending controversies and disruptions concerning EyeCom and the control of and purposes for its collected biometric data. There is a photograph of the Presidential Procession as it tours rain-ravaged areas in the Middle East, a short article about the Wheel and its value as a moving landmark of the city, and a collection of pictures and gossip on the Society page. I leaf through from beginning to end. There is nothing at all about the institute.

Carefully I wash the mug and take a last walk around the apartment. I have lived here, alone, for five years. I am lucky to have it, because the location and the view make it very expensive. The building is prime real estate, they say in the ads.

For the first two years after I walked out of my father's house, determined to make it on my own, I lived in a horrible little hovel in the west end of the city. Its hallways, always dirty and full of drafts, smelled of grease and urine; the stained walls were so thin, they constantly echoed with the yelling and screaming of other tenants. Still, I was determined to make it without Father's help, so it wasn't until I came home from another unsuccessful day of job-hunting one late afternoon to a pried-open door and ravaged, ruined belongings that I finally relented and admitted I could not live like that, after all.

Once again I returned to the house, this time unable to look Father in the eye, fully expecting his rage. But I needn't have; he only nodded, his lined face set, and set about transferring credits to my account without hesitation. He gave me the key to one of the corporate apartments supplied to businessmen through his firm, no questions asked. It was as though he had expected me to fail once again. And I guess I had. Credits continued to be transferred automatically every month, enough to cover all my expenses and more, and even though I had told him I would pay him back as soon as I could, we both knew I wouldn't be able to on a salary from Cosmos Coffee Shop.

I used what I needed and tried sending the rest of it back to him. But the credits kept coming anyway, and I let them pile up in the bank. I could imagine my name being relegated to Father's list of monthly bills, his bookkeeper checking my name off after the utilities. Once again, my father had the upper hand. We had both given up on me.

Now there is nothing more to do, so I take a last look at my view beyond the balcony doors before I close them and pull the shade down. As I leave and ride down the elevator, I wonder if my journey will be a success or if something will go wrong—if I will ever see this apartment again.

Dr. Weiss is just like I have imagined him to be: thin and almost bald with a receding chin and large, round, gray eyes. They are the kind of eyes that would have needed thick glasses, back when such things existed. I know this from all the health documentaries shown us in school. Occasionally he takes a handkerchief from the pocket of his worn white lab coat and mops his bald head with it, which seems bathed in a perpetual shine. Although it's not necessary for him to lose his hair, he has the aura about him of one so fully focused upon his career that he simply does not consider his own physical appearance to be of any significance at all. This is a real rarity, and I find him intriguing. I listen carefully to what he is telling me.

The Kinetic Regression Transport—which he reverently calls Krate—is almost primed for me. It is a long and complicated process and if I am not prepared to go when it's time, the whole thing will have to be aborted and begun again. It is too costly and too risky to mess up. Dr. Weiss tells me these things and more, slowly and carefully, so I will remember them.

"Time regression is similar to riding the Wheel, which is actually two wheels in one: the outer metallic wheel, and the inner glass one. People ascend the ramp and enter the inner glass wheel. When the Wheel begins to move, the inner glass wheel—the one with all the people in it—rotates one way, and the outside wheel rotates the other. Right now, you and I are both riding on the glass one, if you will, traveling toward the future. What the Krate does is take all of your unique readings which it derives from EyeCom—both energy and organic—and transports you to the other wheel. When that is accomplished, you are still moving forward, but in the opposite direction. Then it 'drops you off' at the predetermined place in time—and there you are. As soon as Krate deposits you, you automatically begin riding on the glass wheel once again, although from a different point in time, because that is the natural order of things.

"Retrieval is more complicated. When you are ready to come home, EyeCom makes allowance for any altered bio readings but recognizes your original energy signature. Then the transporter acts like a proverbial bungee cord, bringing you home very quickly."

Dr. Weiss continues with his basic introduction to time travel, most of which I don't understand, but he is adamant about the care I must take while I am there. I must not cause any major rift in the lives of those with whom I come into contact. I must not interfere with major decisions that are made by those people or events that result from such decisions. Small impacts from my presence in the past cannot be avoided, but will be forgiven and smooth themselves over naturally, I am told, due to the constant fabrications of new dimensions where anything that can happen, does. But that, he says, is another lesson for another day.

I will be able to be in limited contact with Dr. Weiss and/or Dr. Moore at least once through my communicator, which I will carry on my person at all times. I must attempt to report any problems or significant observations as soon as possible. I must not reveal the true nature of my presence to anyone, as it could be detrimental and possibly cause panic.

"It's time to give you specific information about the target entity that has been identified by EyeCom," he says.

This is what I have been waiting for.

"Our destination is Port William, North Carolina, Saturday morning, May 5, 1973."

I cannot help but shake my head, incredulous. "It's so long ago," I say. "I don't know anything about such a world."

Dr. Weiss's thin lips draw into a patient smile. "Don't worry, Sera. Remember your history classes from school—they'll come in handy. Just imagine that you don't have any modern convenience except for the barest minimum. It will be like staying at a campground. You'll be fine."

Dr. Moore takes over. "Now listen carefully, Sera. The entity you will find is a young female named Melissa James, twenty-five years old."

I interrupt. "The same age I am now, and the same dates, although on different days of the week—a coincidence?"

"Not at all. Although it's possible to do otherwise, by synchronizing the exact times and dates—present and past—your regression will be much more aligned and safe. We couldn't have asked for better timing. As I said before, I was very much aware of this certain opportunity to hit it all just right, but I would have let it go by, if not for such pressing circumstances in your life."

"Tell me about my past entity. Who is she?"

"On this date in the year 1973, she and her husband Gabe and their two small children reside in a trailer park on the outskirts of town, just up from the beach. Gabe James was a high school jock before some kind of automobile accident, and now he gets around in a wheelchair and cares for their two children. Melissa is a hairdresser, and 'brings home the bacon,' as they used to say."

"How can you know all this about people who lived over two hundred years ago?" I am skeptical, even as I realize I am relieved that my target entity is not male.

"EyeCom is filled with information salvaged from all eras. Back in 2120, so many irreplaceable nondigital historical records were destroyed by the great flood that it was deemed extremely important to keep a large central record, safe from all possible disasters, save a direct hit of a comet with the Earth. It took many years and a lot of hard work to compile the existing databanks from recovered books, mud-smeared courthouse records, newspapers, and private journals—anything from which information could be gleaned. It, along with our present records, is all contained within EyeCom, the main part of which, as you know, lies safely underground in an earthquake-protected area. It is the most complete Hall of Records that has ever existed." She appears impressed by her own facts.

"Even so," Dr. Weiss interjects, tiny beads of sweat breaking out on his bald head, "we do not have everything. Unfortunately, there are still holes in the data where information could not be reclaimed, especially on the east coast where the loss was so profound. But we have enough for your use in this project." He removes a worn handkerchief from his lab coat and swipes absently at his forehead, checks the time on his data wristband, and continues.

"I will give you a readout to study containing all pertinent information—names, address, all the history we have on this family unit, especially Melissa. You will have to fill in the blanks and report back to us so we can add it to the databank. Krate will deposit you at a suitable location within walking distance of the residence. You can use your databand to find it."

Now Dr. Moore leans forward and puts her hand on mine. I am startled. She has never touched me before. I am not used to being touched. "Sera, you will have only twenty-four hours in which to make contact and observe. Even EyeCom has limits, and after that amount of time, your energy signature can become distorted, making it extremely difficult for Krate to retrieve you. Any longer than twenty-four hours, and it could become impossible. We would lose you altogether. EyeCom would read your energy signature as one existing solely in the past."

"Then couldn't it bring me back as if it was bringing someone from the past into the future?"

Dr. Weiss shakes his head, swiping at it again. "There's the rub," he says. "We cannot retrieve a past entity to the future. Anyone who lived and died in the past cannot be brought here. The signatures of past entities and present entities are inherently different in ways that make it impossible. As Dr. Moore said, you would be lost to us forever. You would have to remain in the past, which could have all kinds of repercussions. It would be unacceptable. It's all about balance, you see."

I want to ask him what he means by that, but Dr. Moore moves in. "Most important of all to you is this one newspaper article." She picks up a printout and hands it to me.

It is a copy of an article from *The Port William Herald*, dated Monday, May 7, 1973.

An unidentified woman was pulled from the Waterway near the Oak Island Bridge late Sunday afternoon. A local fisherman spotted the body, which was washed up on the bank under the bridge, and immediately notified local authorities. Police are investigating.

I turn the paper over in my hands. "That's all there is about her death? Isn't there an update or something?"

The doctors glance at each other and then back at me, and shake their heads. "That's all there is," Dr. Moore says.

"It isn't much to go on, you know." I stare at the article again, my brow crinkling. "There's not even a picture?"

"Not a one," Dr. Weiss says. "I'm sorry."

I nod, setting the paper down slowly. "So I guess this is one of those data holes you were talking about?"

They both nod. Dr. Weiss takes a last swab at his head and shoves the handkerchief back into his lab coat. "EyeCom says Melissa James is a positive I.D. To put it simply, she carries your same energy signature, although it's not as strong as yours—she lives in the past. She *is* the target entity. That much we know, and that's the important thing. We know when her energy signature becomes altered—Sunday at 10:15 a.m.—so we must assume that's her time of death. But as for exactly what happened to her, we just don't know."

"It will be up to you to find out," says Dr. Moore. She seems relaxed, as though she has utter confidence. I think it must be part of being a therapist, this exuding of assurance. It's something I haven't learned.

I stand up and walk around the table to the window. The air inside the room is too warm and I wish I were standing out in the cool rain instead. It's hard to breathe.

"What if EyeCom happens to be wrong about one little thing? What if something goes wrong with Krate and it decides it wants me to take an afternoon stroll on Saturn?"

Dr. Moore comes up quietly behind me and puts her hand on my shoulder. "Are you all right, Sera?"

"No," I say. "I'm afraid."

"You know no one is forcing you to do this, don't you?"

I push my damp hair from my face, not answering.

"You have to know that, although this is a complicated thing, this traveling back to the past, it has been done many, many times before, and it is safe. I believe in EyeCom; I believe in Krate, and I honestly think this could help you. If I thought you would be in any real danger, I would tell you not to go and give your money back immediately. And I will, if that's your decision."

Her hand squeezes my shoulder. "Sera, I'm saying you can still abort this regression, and no one will blame you."

I shake my head. The Wheel has begun to roll, and I'm getting on for the ride this time. "No way," I tell her. "I'm going."

Wednesday, May 5, 2202

10:10 a.m.

I'm reclining comfortably on the broad, gray chair inside Krate. The chair is squishy-soft, like a cloud. There is no need to be strapped in, and it is as though I am relaxing on my own sofa at home, only better. With my okay, Dr.

Moore has given me a light tranquilizer, which already softens the hard edges of apprehension.

Krate is actually a small room with a narrow observation window running down one side. The walls are all white, and the lighting is muted and low. There are no visible panels or buttons as I had imagined there would be—only the chair and a single holographic poster on the wall that I am now facing. It displays a lovely, primeval forest. Trees stand tall, their trunks covered with rough, black bark. Clouds of light green leaves engulf their graceful, winding boughs; tangled roots disappear into rich, dark loam from which rises a stand of delicate ferns, still coiled at their tips. I can almost smell the damp earth and hear the high call of a mockingbird taking respite among the branches. Now I see a path; it begins in the foreground, winds its way around the trees—but I cannot see the other end of it. *It is lost in the wood.*

My hands lie relaxed on the soft, cushioned arms of the chair. Low, peaceful music wafts around me, its source undetectable. I can see Dr. Weiss. He stands beyond the small window, his expression calm. Dr. Moore stands beside me. She makes sure I have my bag buckled securely to my waist, the one that contains the few items I am allowed to take with me. The bag is made of suede leather with a long fringe running along its bottom seam. I am dressed in scratchy denim pants, which flare curiously out over my leather boots. My white, silky blouse is pulled down around my shoulders, the sleeves loose but elasticized at the wrists. It is a peasant blouse, I have been told. This is the best they can do for me. I will have to buy anything else that I need.

I am as prepared for the journey as is possible, and Dr. Moore declares me ready to go as she exits the room and shuts the door behind her. I see her face appear in the observation window alongside that of Dr. Weiss, who gives a thumbs-up—Krate is also ready.

I wonder if I should close my eyes, but I don't. I want to see what is happening. Now a humming begins—a deep, bass humming that I can feel in my back and chest, as well as hear. I focus upon the forest and breathe deeply. The low vibrations move around me and through me, and they seem to bend back upon themselves, echoing off each other.

Now it is as though I have been propelled in my chair—shot—into a light as bright, as all-consuming, as the sun. Only there is no heat, and no sound at all—only a silence more profound than I have ever known. I can no longer see the walls of the room or the observation window. The light wraps around my eyes, my mind; even though I do not seem to be moving, I sense that I am moving very fast—faster than is possible.

I am balanced on the crest of a great wave, riding it toward something wondrous . . .

2

Lissa

Friday, May 4, 1973

If Bug blows out them candles one more time, I'm gonna scream. There ain't much left to them, 'cause I've used them at least twice before, once for Gabe's birthday and—let's see . . . I guess for my own. Yeah, I had to bake my own damned birthday cake. You'd just as soon see a Chinese cow fly over as see anybody lift a finger for anything in my house.

Sure enough, there the little shit goes, crawling up in the chair and sticking his little tow head right up to the flames, puffing up his cheeks like as if that's the right way to inhale. He lets loose with a blast of air from his lips that sounds more like a sick fart.

"Stop! Bug, you stop spittin' on the cake right now," I yell at him, and his face crinkles up like I knew it would.

"I wanna bwow out da candows," he whines, tears streaking the dirt on his cheeks.

"Well, you can't till it's your own birthday, and that ain't for—what? Ten more months. Now get down off the chair, and Hailey, you come on around the table over here and hurry up and blow these things out. Lookit that—they're about melted down to nothing. Hurry up."

Hailey's been sucking her thumb again even though I dipped it in red pepper sauce this morning. It's all white and pruney and wet. She walks so slow around the table she must think it's made of dynamite. She's got seven candles on the chocolate cake this time; you'd think she'd be happy to blow them out. She has got to be the most skittish little thing I ever saw. Ever time I tell her something she gets that dazed, deer-caught-in-the-headlights look to her. I always have to push her to do this, push her to do that. She's slow as Christmas, too. If we're all sitting at the supper table eating, she picks and picks at her food till the rest of us are finished, even Bug. Then I have to yell at her to hurry up and get through so I can wash her plate or else she'd be sitting there all night, I guess.

Course, I always have to do all the yelling around here, 'cause you know Gabe ain't gonna take the initiative to do anything. When the kids start up he just sets there in his chair and acts the cripple, cutting his eyes at me like I'm the bad person when I have to discipline them. *His* kids—they are just as much his as mine, but does he help make it any easier on me? No sir, he don't, not at all.

Well, Herself has made it to the candles and one of them has gone out because it melted into the icing. She peeks over at Gabe and he smiles at her and nods, and she finally inhales and blows out the rest of them. Gabe laughs and claps; Hailey claps too.

Bug sniffles and climbs up on the chair again. "I want some boofday cake, Mama, an' some ice cweem in it," he says, nodding.

"All right, all right; thank God Hailey finally put us all out of our misery. Gabe, would you cut the cake while I get the ice cream. Bug, sit down. Hailey, scrape them candles off the icing."

I shove open the swinging door to the kitchen and let it whoosh closed behind me. I can hear them on the other side, busying themselves. "My baby girl is seven years old," I hear Gabe say announcer-like to Hailey, and I know she's gushing with her daddy's sudden attention. She adores him.

"I wanna have sebin candows on *my* boofday cake, too," Bug is saying, and I can tell he's already stuffed some into his mouth.

"You got to work up to it, big guy," Gabe says. "Next time you'll get four, then the next time five, and so on. Some day—man, you'll have so many candles on your birthday cake, you won't be able to blow them all out by yourself. You'll have to hire people off the street and get them in here to help—a *whole crowd* of them." Bug is laughing now, a muffled cake laugh, and Hailey is giggling.

I lean against the cabinet, rub my aching forehead, and dig around in the drawer for the ice cream scoop. All I want to do is get this damn cake eaten and the mess cleaned up and the kids to bed and then I'm going out. I've earned it.

* * *

Gabe is in the kids' room reading Hailey's favorite bedtime story out loud, the one about a fairy princess that goes to sleep and wakes up after being kissed by a handsome prince. Bug usually whines until Gabe gives up and reads them the one with the dragon in it instead, but it's Hailey's big day and Bug is half asleep anyway.

I'm worn out after scrubbing icing and wax out of everything—including Bug's hair—and getting the kids' baths done and such. Hailey wanted to play with her new Barbie awhile, but I told her it was already past bedtime so she put the doll in a shoebox bed she'd fixed up with sewing scraps and told it, "Night-night, sleep tight, don't let the bedbugs bite," like her Granny does to her. You want to see somebody spoil the shit out of a kid, it's my mother. Any time they spend a couple nights over at her house, it takes a week to get them straight again. And you better believe she hears about it from me. But does she care if she makes it harder on me? No sir. It's just a good thing for me she lives in Georgia.

I stand in front of the bathroom mirror that's still foggy from my shower to brush my damp hair, and wonder should I put it up on top of my head, or let it stay down around my shoulders, straight like the other girls wear it? It's shiny and auburn, my best feature, according to Gabe. I decide to leave it down. I pull a green sundress with spaghetti straps over my head and smooth it down over my hips. The hemline hangs several inches above my knees. The scooped neckline shows off a little cleavage. I'm proud of my figure. Sure, I gained weight with the kids, but I starved myself back down to one-fifteen again each time, and it wasn't easy, either.

When I was in elementary school, I was the fat kid. I ain't gonna say I was humongous, but I had all this extra baby fat, and Papa used to bring home treats for his little girl like candy bars and shit that I couldn't resist, and that didn't help, either. At school some of the boys called me "Boom-Boom Girl" 'cause they said that was the sound I made walking down the hall. And they would make oinking noises in the cafeteria while I was sitting alone, trying to eat my lunch. To them I wasn't a person; I was an object—a target for their cruel fat jokes. I hated them.

At night, in bed, I'd think of all kinds of ways to hurt them bad and make them sorry they ever tangled with me. My favorite torture was one I read about somewhere called the copper bowl. You tie a person down so they can't move, and strap a copper bowl bottom side up over his abdomen, and put a hungry rat under it. Then you light a little fire on top of the bowl so it gets real hot, and the only way that rat has to escape the heat from the bowl is to eat its way down through the person's intestines.

The girls weren't much better. Most of the time they'd just ignore me, and whenever it came time to choose sides for kickball at recess, they'd leave me for last and whichever team got stuck with me would roll their eyes and put me at the end of the line to kick, 'cause I couldn't run very fast or kick very far. More often than not, I'd be crying when I got home from school, and when I'd tell Mama what was wrong, she'd tell me I was beautiful and fix me a heaping plate of macaroni and cheese for dinner, which was my favorite.

Then around the seventh grade I got my period and started filling out, and that's when the baby fat went away and those same boys I'd pass in the hall that used to tease me started looking at me in a real different way. Of course, to them I was still just an object—them sneers just turned to leers.

At first I felt self-conscious of my extra-big boobs, tiny waist, and full hips, but then as I noticed how boys would act kind of goofy and flustered around me in class, I began to see I had a special kind of power over them. I learned to flirt and joke with them to get what I wanted—little things at first, like snacks and pens and gum. Then as I got older and filled out even more, I got things like free lunches and rides to school and answers to test questions. I didn't even have to go all the way, either. If a boy was especially good to me, I might let him cop a feel or something in the movie theatre, but that was all. Just enough to drive him crazy for more. That was my power.

The popular girls still ignored me, but I told myself they were just stupid, envious little bitches and that I had all the attention I needed anyway. The only girls I cared to hang around with were Cindy and Becka. Cindy was always kind of weird and shit, and Becka was a nerdy bookworm. In a way we were our own club of misfits.

Now I smile at myself in the mirror. I just happen to care about the way I look, unlike some people. Take Gabe, for instance. Every morning he dresses in the same old, worn-out, holey jeans and tee shirts. If he were to pull a comb through his hair, it would be a true cause for fireworks. I mean, he don't smell or nothing—he keeps himself clean, all right—but he looks like a street bum. I used to ask him, "Would it kill you to fix up once in a while?" But he just don't care, so I finally gave up.

I pull on some tall brown boots and hang my gold necklace around my neck. It ain't real gold. Gabe gave it to me for Christmas, but I might as well wear it now, since *we* never go out or nothing. I grab my pocketbook off the bed, and I'm ready to go.

I figure Gabe is gonna raise a stink, but I don't care. He comes out of the kids' bedroom into the little hallway the same time I'm coming out of our bedroom, and we both stop short. He looks me up and down. "What are you doing, Lissa?"

I pull the strap of my bag over my shoulder. "I'm going out and meet the girls at the Diner. Becka and Cindy."

He frowns. "Well, I was just thinking, since it was Hailey's birthday today—since we had a little party and all—well, I was just feeling like it would be good to spend a nice evening here together. Just us."

I look at him in his tattered clothes, setting there in that wheelchair. "And do what?" I walk around him and go on into the kitchen where I can get my keys and go.

He follows behind me like a puppy. "I don't know—pop some popcorn and watch a movie on TV." He laughs a little. "Remember when we used to sit at the coffee table and play Scrabble half the night? Remember that? And after that we could fool around some. It's been a while, Lissa."

I grab the car keys off the kitchen counter and spin around on him. "It's *Friday night*, Gabe," I yell at him. "Don't you get it? I am on my feet at the beauty parlor for all hours of the day and bring home dinner and bake a damn birthday cake and clean up after all three of you, and I deserve to get out. Other people are out there right now, dancing, partying, and having a good time after a long, hard workweek—something *you* wouldn't know anything about—and here we are, stuck in this shithole because you never want to go out and meet anybody or do anything new. Well, I don't know about you, but I'm too young to just give up and die."

If it was anybody else, they would tell me goodbye and good riddance, or at least be yelling back at me or something. But no, he takes my hand and holds it in both of his. His face looks pinched, like somebody knocked him in the head or something. "Well, what are you all gonna do, Lissa—you and Becka and Cindy?"

"I don't know," I say slowly and deliberately. "Talk, I guess. Have a couple Cokes. Listen to Cindy's gossip and Becka's stupid jokes."

"*We* could talk," he says, and whips his head around like he's looking for something, then his eyes light up. "We'll do something crazy—I'll play the guitar and you can sing, like we used to do in high school. I just put a new string on it and got it tuned up and all. It'll be fun."

I feel like screaming when he does this—acts all clingy and whiny. It makes me sick to look at him. Sick. I pull my hand back from him and my pocketbook strap falls off my shoulder so I yank it back up again.

"Quit whinin', Gabe," is all I can think of to say to him. I walk out the back door to the VW bus. I half expect him to follow me outside, but he don't. Thank God for small favors.

One of the headlights is out in the VW bus again. I ain't surprised—something or other is always broke on it, then I have to shell out my hard-earned money to fix it. If I was to set down and figure out how long it was I had to stand on my feet with my hands tangled up in some fat ole biddy's blue hair just to pay for everything gone bad on that damn bus, I'd probably bust a gut.

What I'd like is that little red convertible Mustang down at the Sand Dollar Used Car Lot. What a cool looking car. I can see me tooling down 211, top down—me in a cute little sundress, wearing my fancy straw hat with the red ribbon tied under my chin and my hair blowing out from under it, and the aviator's sunglasses Becka gave me, the ones her brother who's in the Air Force accidentally left in her car on his furlough. *That* would make a few heads turn.

But no, we have to have something that's big enough for two kids and a wheelchair to fit in the back, and all the other shit like groceries and such. And anyway, I'm sure I don't have the money to buy it. Some kid will snap it up with his daddy's money before you know it, and wrap it around a tree or something. Damn waste of a good car, if you ask me.

I'm just glad to get out of that armpit of a house and breathe some fresh air for awhile. Whenever I'm alone and get a few miles down the road, I feel this huge load dropping off me—like as if I've been lugging around a big basket of sopping wet laundry on my back all day, and now I've just unloaded it at the curb and left it behind. I turn up the radio 'cause Carly Simon's singing "You're So Vain." I love music, just about any kind.

Gabe is always fiddling around on that stupid guitar of his, but he can't play worth shit. Sure, I thought it was cool when we first started going out and all. He even played lead guitar in a little band for a while. They weren't very good, but it was kind of fun to listen to them, even though they had a lame name like The Manic Mushroom. There was just the three of them—Gabe on guitar, David on drums, and Andy on bass. They used to practice in David's parents' garage with the door pulled down so the neighbors wouldn't complain. Sometimes I'd get Cindy and Becka and we'd set inside on folding chairs and watch them. Once in a while they'd even let me hold a microphone and sing. They'd crank up the amps and we'd do "Louie Louie" like you wouldn't believe.

For a while I had a huge crush on Andy because he was quiet and had these big dark eyes. But he had a girlfriend, Alison. Man, was she spaced out, too. Always smiling and hanging on him like a leech. She had stringy, dishwater-blond hair and stuck little silver gummed stars on her face, and always wore these long strings of beads that clicked against each other every time she moved—it used to drive me crazy. He used to look at me plenty, although I never let on I knew. One time when Alison was home sick, Andy cornered me in the garage when nobody was looking and asked me did I want to go to the Crescent Drive-in with him that night. I told him it depended on what was showing, and he said if we went to the movie there'd be plenty showing, all right. Thing of it was, once I knew I could have him, I didn't really want him. So I said I was busy.

Gabe was all right, I guess. He wasn't a cripple back then, in high school. He was pretty athletic. He was a forward on the school basketball team, and I used to sit in the bleachers and watch him play. He was good, too; he'd dribble that ball and dodge around all them other guys and first thing you know—*wham!* He'd dunk it through that hoop like it was nothing. Everybody'd go crazy, jumping up and yelling, and I'd sit there feeling flushed and special, 'cause after a while

I was wearing his jacket. He probably could've got a scholarship; people said he was that good.

Since I didn't hang with the popular kids at school, it was lucky for me Gabe moved from a different state so he didn't know my fat kid history. To him I had always been pretty. I'd only come close to going all the way a few times, but I decided Gabe was different. I could see some real possibilities in him, what with his athletic talent. Gabe and I started dating hot and heavy, our senior year. He gave me his class ring and I wrapped tape around it so it would fit my finger. During the day he'd carry my books at school; evenings we'd fog up the windows of his father's Dodge. So it's easy to see why I ended up pregnant and married, in that order, two months before graduation. But we had us a plan. Gabe was gonna work part-time and go to college and play basketball, and I was gonna cut hair part-time and raise the baby. We were young and stupid and we thought the world was ours.

Then one rainy night, Gabe and a couple of guys piled into Wes Wilson's Fairlane to go grab a burger after a game, and as far as anybody could figure, that idiot Wes must have got the bright idea to drag race with some other dumb-ass at the intersection of Merritt and South. They ended up flipped over in a ditch. Nobody was wearing a seatbelt, of course. Wes and another guy was both declared dead at the scene; one guy ended up in a coma and never come out of it; Gabe broke his back and was paralyzed in both legs. At the time, they said he was the lucky one, but I don't know.

All my life, I ain't had the things other girls at school had: pretty new clothes, pink canopy beds, stacks of records and tapes—I could go on and on. My parents and I lived in a shitty little hole-in-the-wall house on the edge of town. If you was to stand on the porch and spit, that's about as much land as they had, too, with all them other little box houses sitting in a row. Papa and Mama both worked in the mill and they acted like they was proud of it. But they didn't have to go to school every day like me, and see how other people lived in the real world. I was ashamed of how we lived. And when Papa died the year I was to turn sweet sixteen, I was even ashamed of the way he died, dropping dead of a heart attack like he did, right over the machine at the mill. I was mad at him 'cause he'd worked himself to death. I refused to cry at the funeral. Mama just thought I was being brave.

All I wanted was for Gabe to make it big, like he ought to have. You see, I'd already had it all planned out in my head. If only he could have gotten that basketball scholarship and made the pros, *man*, we would have had it made. We'd be floating in money and living in a huge house in some big city like Atlanta, and I'd be living like a queen. I'd have me a walk-in closet filled with all the latest fashions, and a cook to make all our meals, and a maid to do all the cleaning, and a nanny to take care of the kids, and I'd be a member of some bridge club or something and do a pictorial interview for *Redbook Magazine* as the wife of a famous basketball star . . .

Anyway, it's been a long time from there to here, and I'm sick to death of thinking about what coulda been. I hate to say it, but I've come to accept my lot in life, and I'll move on. You gotta keep growing. I have decided that if I'm gonna have any excitement at all, I'd better make my own—and I plan to, sure as shit. The person I am back at the trailer is flat, like a cardboard cutout. But there's more to Melissa James than meets the eye. I've grown that way. Someday I'm gonna move on.

I can see the lights of Oak Island Diner ahead on the right. It looks still as death tonight, only a few cars parked on the side. I drive right by it, and go on a few miles across the bridge and then a few more; I turn right at the 7-Eleven, head on down the narrow, winding road toward the water, and turn in to the Riverview Bar & Grille, tires crunching on the gravel drive. I can hear the thump-thump of music all the way out here, so you know it's gotta be loud inside.

I walk in and the jukebox is screaming out "Reeling in the Years" by Steely Dan. There's a thick cloud of smoke suspended in the air, like early morning mist hanging over the Cape Fear River. The only thing louder than the music is the people, shouting to be heard over their own noise. Glasses are clinking at the bar; people are setting on the stools and in the booths and at the tables and milling around, all crowded up like a bunch of hogs. Finally I see Cindy's bleached out hair poking up through the mist, and sure enough, Becka is sitting beside her. Somehow they've managed to get a booth over near the bar. They've spotted me too, and are wildly waving me over. There's already a few empty Bud bottles on their table, and the two of them are laughing and their faces are flushed. I could venture to say they're already headed toward a good buzz.

Cindy raises her bottle and takes a good gulp, and wipes her mouth with the back of her hand. "Where you *been*, Lissa?"

Becka nods her frizzy red head as she pops a couple of peanuts into her mouth. I look down and the bowl is about empty. "You got a lot of catchin' up to do, kid," she says. Neither one of them is dressed up. They got on tee shirts and jeans, just like everybody else. I'm the only class act here, I guess, but I'm used to that.

Cindy and Becka and me go back a long ways. It was Cindy and me first, then in the eighth grade Becka moved from California, and we three just clicked for some reason. Cindy was always the reckless one, Becka was more quiet and polite, and me, I was just kind of middle of the road, I guess, as likely to go one way as the other. That was back then. Now Cindy works at a bank and Becka is a nurse's assistant at the hospital. We've all three of us seen a lot of changes and stuck together through all of them. Cindy is my listening post, though. I tell Cindy things I wouldn't tell Becka, on account of she may not approve. I guess Becka ain't no angel or nothing, but Cindy and I share more perspectives on things.

Gabe can't stand her 'cause I'm more likely to tell her stuff than I am him. He probably knows that half the time, I'm complaining about him.

"I told y'all it was Hailey's birthday. I had to do the cake thing and clean up and all that shit. Then Gabe gives me a hard time about going out—you know, the usual." I set down on the other side of the booth and dig a half-pack of Marlboros out of my bag. Gabe don't like the smell on me, but I can always blame it on Cindy, who smokes like a chimney. I ain't gonna set here and drink beer without smoking cigarettes. Cindy flicks her lighter and I inhale deep. I feel the dizzy relief I get when I light up after a long time. It helps put things into perspective. I pick up a beer and down half of it, I'm so thirsty.

"Did he get mad?" Becka is saying, while Cindy jumps up to go get us more beers.

"I don't know. Some," I say, looking through the crowd. "It don't matter; I'm here, ain't I?"

Becka giggles, her eyes watery and blinking from the beer and the smoke. "What did you get Hailey for her birthday?"

I look at her. "A Barbie doll, and some shorts and a top. Mama sent her a science book."

"A *science* book?"

"Yeah, it's got stuff about the ocean in it. Pictures and shit."

Becka nods, all dreamy looking. "Yeah, that's cool," she says.

"I guess."

Cindy appears through the mob and plunks herself down along with some cold beers. I grab one up and take a long drink. Gabe's gonna smell beer on me now, too, which they don't exactly serve at the Diner. I guess I can say Cindy had some in her car and made me sip some. He'll believe that.

"Guess who's slumming?" she says, jerking her thumb toward the bar and grinning like a jack-o-lantern. "You ain't gonna believe it, Lissa." She lights up one of my Marlboros for herself.

"I don't know, who is it?"

"Who's the last guy you'd expect to see at a bar on a Friday night, *alone*?"

I have to play her game or she'll never tell me. "Uh . . . Roger Peters? Bill Case? *Elvis Presley? Donald Duck?*"

Cindy is grinning and shaking her head like she's got strings attached at both ends and somebody's yankin' on them. It's driving me crazy. "I don't know, just tell me," I say to her.

Becka giggles.

Cindy leans up close, like as if she's gonna whisper it to me, but she has to yell anyway. "Brian Kelly," she says, and waits for my reaction, her eyes big.

"You're full of shit," I say.

Becka strains her neck to peer through the crush of people at the bar, but she doesn't say anything.

"No I ain't, either," Cindy says. "He's up there talking with a couple of guys, sitting on the stools, and there's no Marie in sight. It's just like I heard—him and Marie are separated."

I can't help myself; I have to look over to the bar, just like Becka. And there he sits, Big Brian, all six feet of him—hair black as coal, deep blue eyes, strong jaw, broad shoulders, hard-muscled arms—every gorgeous male bit of him. Man, what a hunk.

Back in high school he was a football star, class president. His grades weren't so great, but who cared. Him and Marie were together even back then; she was a cheerleader and all, so they were like a matched set. Everybody knew they would get married someday and he would carry on his father's appliance business, and they would have a family and own a house in the finer section of Port William forever.

"Well, that doesn't mean they've split up, just 'cause he's sitting here alone at the bar on Friday night," Becka says. "Maybe he just needed to get out of the house."

Cindy and I look at each other and laugh.

"You are so naïve, Becka—I swear you are," Cindy says. She runs a hand through her short bleached hair and it falls immediately back into place. "Now, you know Marie ain't gonna let him outa her sight unless something's very wrong. She's had that man wrapped around her finger so tight all these years, he couldn't turn to piss."

"I ain't never seen a man so whipped," I say, agreeing with her. I'd seen him and her in Kroger sometimes—her walking around picking out stuff, and him pushing the cart along with the baby in it, and he just had that whipped air about him. "Wow, if they really split up, it must have been over something big. Wonder what happened?"

Cindy lifts her bottle and takes a big swallow. "Well, I heard they have fights over money. She's so damn controlling it ain't funny, but he spends it on booze and pot and gambling. I think she finally kicked him out over some major bet he lost playing poker. Heard she threw all his clothes out into the yard one night and locked him out. She's even selling his boat."

Becka sighs real big and pushes her empty bottle away. "*Geez*, he's so cute. Remember how all us girls wanted to date him in junior high? But Marie got her claws in him and wouldn't let go. She was so jealous of him."

"Yeah, what a bitch," I say. "One time I dropped a book in the hall and the two of them happened to be passing by, so he bent over and picked it up for me, and she about had a conniption, grabbing his arm and steering him off like she was leading a farm animal to slaughter or something, all the time gabbing and pretending she didn't see me standing there."

We grab another bowl of nuts, drink more beers, and shoot the shit for awhile. People keep feeding the jukebox and it goes through so many songs one after the other that they all run together into one big medley of Led Zeppelin, Doobie Brothers, Elton John, James Brown, and on and on. I can feel myself relaxing like I haven't for what seems like ages, and don't it feel *good*. Cindy is leaning back against the booth and I can tell she's pretty sloshed. I'm starting to feel a buzz myself, halfway through my third beer.

I look at Cindy. She ain't a beauty queen, but she's kind of cute in her own way, and I get a notion. "Why don't you go over there and ask him to dance?" I say to her, nodding toward Brian.

A strange look comes over her face and then she cracks up, her shoulders bobbing. "Me? Hell, no. Any girl gets messed up with him is just asking for trouble."

Becka gets up to head for the ladies' room. Her eyes are bloodshot and she's kind of weaving.

"Not if Marie is out of the picture, right?" I say, looking around for more peanuts. "He's probably all depressed and lonely and horny." I grin at her and dig one peanut up from the bowl and slowly suck the salt off it.

Cindy laughs again, but she's shaking her head. "Marie ain't never gonna be out of the picture. That's the kind of girl, when she kicks her old man out, *she* don't want him, but she don't want nobody else to have him, neither. And he's so whipped he'll be like the Doberman in that corner fenced lot on Magnolia and Coral—you know, the one that barks his head off and charges like he wants to tear you apart if you're walking by? But soon as he *does* jump over the fence he gets this spooked, confused look on his face like he don't know what to do, and he jumps *right back over*, and starts up barking again. I seen him do it more than once." She jerks her head in the bar's direction. "That's what he's gonna be like. He wouldn't know what to do with a girl if he got one, it's probably been so long."

I'm looking over at Brian through the smog and to my surprise, I get tingly all over. Maybe it's the beer, maybe it's curiosity, or maybe it's just plain old wanting something I know I can't have, but all of a sudden, I want him. I want him bad.

Cindy knows me pretty well, 'cause she kicks me under the table. "Girl, you better watch out," she says. "I seen that look in your eye before."

"I'm all grown up, Cindy-girl. I can do what I want, and ain't nobody gonna tell me what I can't have."

"You tell that to Gabe."

I look at her. "Since when are you on Gabe's side?"

"Since never. But what if he were to find out?" She lays her hands down flat on the table in front of her. "You know I don't care what you do, Lissa—I've covered for you plenty of times before. Hell, I'm happy to do it, and you've done the same for me. But Brian's hands-off. You get messed up with him, and you'll be in way over your head. He's out of our league. That's all I'm saying."

Becka slides in beside Cindy and she looks even paler than usual, which is saying something. I got white sheets at home, got more color than that girl. "You all right, Becka?"

She nods and sniffs and stares at the bowl of peanuts. "It's too stuffy in here, is all," she says. "I ain't feeling so hot. I might need to go home, Cindy. Okay?"

Cindy rolls her eyes so Becka can't see but I can. "Can't you wait till I have one more beer?"

Becka sniffs some more and fiddles with her napkin. I'm betting she barfed in the bathroom. "She ain't feeling good, Cindy," I say. Becka looks up at me, grateful-like.

Cindy downs the swallow of beer that's left in her bottle and gathers up her pocketbook. "All right, let's go," she sighs. "It's getting late anyway." She looks hard at me. "I guess Lissa's about ready to go home too, ain't you, Lissa?"

"Soon. I'm just going to set here and finish this last beer."

Cindy tilts her head at me and makes a face.

"*Really*," I say to her.

"Suit yourself. *Call* me," she says. Becka looks back at me and they disappear into the gloom.

I stretch out my left hand, palm down, stare at the thin silver wedding band, and turn it around and around on my finger. It comes off easy enough, and I slip it into the deep pocket of my dress.

"Bad, Bad Leroy Brown" is playing as I walk up to the bar to get me a fresh beer. I just happen to be standing right next to Brian, who's still perched on a barstool. He doesn't seem too interested in anything going on around him. He's got that sad old puppy dog look to him—a rapidly getting drunk puppy dog. Fortunately the barkeep is busy, so I take out a cigarette and dig around in my bag for some matches, which I find on top but keep digging for anyway. I already know Brian falls for the helpless female thing. But the idiot ain't looking, so I say, "Damn," while I'm digging, to get his attention. It works, of course.

There's a flick and a flame. "Here you go," he says, holding his lighter out to me. I act surprised, cupping my hand lightly around his in order to hold it steady, and puckering my lips while I'm inhaling. It's some of my best stuff, but then, like Cindy says, he's out of our league. So I can't be playing around—I gotta be direct. I let the smoke out, slowly, but I'm still looking at him while he's shoving the lighter back into his pocket. "Thanks," I say.

"Don't mention it."

I smile, and then he smiles.

He ain't exactly busting down the bar to make an effort here, and I'm thinking maybe Cindy was right. Maybe he *don't* know what to do with a girl anymore. Or worse, maybe he just don't find me attractive. Nah, that can't be it. I know I look good in this dress.

"You, uh—you seen a girl with dark hair over here somewhere tonight?" I ask.

He looks around and back at me. "Naw."

"Oh. I was waiting for a friend, but I guess she couldn't make it." I smile and shrug.

He nods and smiles. I'm wondering, does he recognize me from school all those years ago? I'm wondering if I should just give up and walk away while I still got my dignity.

Then he holds out a strong hand. "I'm Doug," he says, still smiling.

I gather he don't have a glimmer of who I am after all, and he's too chicken to use his own name. But I also notice he ain't wearing his wedding ring.

"And I'm Rita. Nice to meet you." I shake hands with him and I'm thinking it's an odd thing to do in a bar—shake hands with a guy like that. His hand is a little clammy, too. Still, he's looking at me with them incredible blue eyes.

"Nights in White Satin" is playing and he asks do I want to dance, and I say, "That'd be nice, Doug."

And even though the dance corner is so crowded you can barely move without getting bumped or stepped on, and you can't say two words without shouting, Brian and I manage to dance away most of that evening like it's just the two of us out there. With the music pounding in my head, I pretend we're teenagers again and I'm popular just like Brian, and all the kids are looking at us like we're the perfect couple. During the slow dances I reach up and put my arms over his shoulders, which causes my short dress to draw up even more, and he slides his hands down over my butt and pulls me up so close to him, till it's more than obvious he's getting some enjoyment out of it, too.

Then before I know it, the bar's closing down.

I head for the ladies' room and when I come out Brian is waiting for me, leaning against the wall near the phones. "You need a ride home, Rita?" he asks.

I forget he doesn't know who I am. For all he knows, I'm single with my own apartment—I *wish*. I wonder where he's staying, but I'm not supposed to know he's married and thrown out of his own house, so I don't ask.

"No, I got my own ride out there . . ." he nods and his face falls a little ". . . but you can come out and set in it with me for awhile, if you want."

Brian may not be the brightest bulb in the fixture, but Cindy was wrong—Brian does remember what to do with a girl. In fact, in the back of my VW bus, he remembers nonstop for twenty minutes before he passes out. One moment he's grinding away, the next moment he's out—no warning, no nothing. He's just lying there on top of me like a downed tree. I finally roll him off and slap him a little, trying to wake him up.

"Hey Doug—get up. Get up. Hey. Brian. *I said wake the hell up.*" Nothing.

I set there with my head in my hands for about ten minutes, trying to think how to fix this mess. 'Cause at this point, I ain't exactly Lucy Lucid, myself. I've had more than my usual share to drink tonight. In fact, the bus seems like it's spinning around like it's caught in a tornado, and I'm not feeling so good. I'm not feeling good at all. I try to make it to the door, but I can't help it—I barf right there all over Brian. "*Dammit,*" I say, wiping my mouth. Now I got two messes to clean up, and all I want to do is go home and go to sleep.

I try to get it together long enough to at least get my clothes put back on. I shove Brian hard and he groans once, but he just won't wake up. All I know is, he sure as hell can't stay here. I push open the side door of the bus and get out, and start pulling on Brian's feet. He's so heavy I can't believe it—I mean, the guy must be made of solid muscle, and I always heard muscle is heavier than fat. I pull and I yank and I cuss and struggle and pull some more, but it ain't working. Then I spy a length of cord Hailey and one of her little friends use as a jump rope sometimes, coiled up in one corner of the bus, like a snake. I ain't surprised. No matter how many times I give them hell about it, the kids are forever leaving shit in here—crayons, toys, and scraps—most of the time it's like a pigsty.

I grab the rope and find Brian's pants in another corner, and dig his keys out of a pocket. I get out of the bus, looking all around to make good and sure nobody's around. Everybody else has already left. I hotfoot it to the only other vehicle left in the parking lot, a big Ford truck. I guess he uses it to haul his boat, which he probably ain't got anymore. God is it ugly—but the key fits the door lock, and I slide into the driver's seat and start her right up.

I back the thing up very carefully till the truck's back bumper is up near the open side door of the bus, put it in park, and leave it idling while I get out and run around and tie one end of the rope to the trailer hitch ball doohickey, and tie the other end around the ankle of one of Brian's boots. Although he's naked, he's still got his boots on. I wonder how in the hell he managed to do that, but only for a second, because I just ain't got the time.

I scamper around and get back in the truck, and slowly push down on the accelerator till I hear a *kerthump* behind me and I'm good and sure Brian is slid out of the bus completely. Then I kill the engine and run back around and untie the rope from the hitch and from his ankle, and pitch it through the door of the bus. I climb up in the bus and grab all his clothes, turn around and throw them in a heap on the ground, and shinny back down, slamming the door of the bus shut behind me.

Then I stand there breathing hard for a moment in the sick yellow glow of the parking lot's one sorry streetlight, looking down at Brian lying there in the gravel. Except for his boots he's stark naked, covered in vomit, and drunker than a brewer's fart. I can't help but feel a little sorry; he probably ain't gonna want to see me again. At least I managed to clean up both messes at the same time. God knows, I've cleaned me up enough messes.

I slide behind the wheel of the bus and hightail it out of the gravel lot, up the winding street, and onto 211, and somehow I manage to make it home. I'm pretty sobered up by this time, what with all the physical torment I've just been through.

The porch light on the trailer's shining as I turn into the drive and I pray Gabe is asleep—I really don't have the energy to make up any excuses as to why I'm so late. But I needn't have worried, 'cause he's lying in bed facing the wall when I slide in next to him, and the little bar he uses to help himself into bed isn't swinging, so he *must* be asleep. It probably takes all of three seconds for me to finally pass out.

I don't remember dreaming or nothing—just the black nothingness of very deep sleep. Then I feel something pulling at my arm and whining like a mosquito right in my ear. I flap at it but it's still a-whining, and I can't make it stop. I open my eyes and see Bug's head in my face.

"Mama," he's saying, "da phone is for yooo." He pulls on my arm again, and his hand is all wet. I don't want to know why. "Giddup, Mama, wite now."

I rub my eyes, my head pounding. I reach out to the nightstand and pick up the phone and say, "I got it," into the receiver, listen for Gabe to hang up in the living room, and hear the click. I glare at Bug until he runs out of the room.

"Lissa, it's me. I'm over at the church."

I don't know how the hell Cindy can sound so lively when I'm feeling like I do now. "What the hell you doing there?" I say. My mouth is smacking like it's full of cotton, it's so dry.

"I'm helping out my Auntie Ada. They're having some kind of supper tonight and I told her I'd help out with the tables and such."

I can feel myself falling back to sleep, I'm so interested.

"Lissa?" she's saying, "What the hell did you do last night?"

I yawn. "I finished my beer."

"Well, is that *all*?"

I smile, my eyes still closed. "Naw, I might have got me another beer."

"Well, you're not gonna believe what I just heard—they found Brian Kelly dead this morning."

A bolt of lightning shoots through me, head to toes, and I set up straight in the bed. "*What* did you say?"

I can tell she's got her hand cupped around the phone. "You should hear the buzz going on around here, Lissa. Apparently Marie Kelly's next door neighbor is Miz Tucker, who relayed the news to Miz Blake, and since she's tight with my Auntie Ada, Miz Blake told her, and—"

"*Cindy. What happened?*"

"Well, they don't know. They say somebody found him early this morning outside the Riverview Bar in the parking lot, buck naked except for his boots, lying behind his truck and dead as a doorstop. Can you imagine that?"

I can. And it's a good thing I'm setting down, because all the blood has drained clean out of my head. "But they don't know anything else?"

"Nobody knows what happened, I guess. The police were out at the bar, of course, and at Marie's house—that's how Miz Tucker found out about it, you know. I think they're waiting for an autopsy report or something. I don't know."

My head is pounding hard as the surf outside. I know he was alive when I left him. Wasn't he?

Bug scampers back into the room and pulls at my arm again. "Giddup, Mama, I'm hungwee. Giddup, I said."

"Stop it, Bug; go tell your dad," I say to him. "*Go on.*" He runs out.

"Cindy," I say quietly into the phone.

"Yeah?"

"Listen to me very carefully. You can't tell anyone we saw Brian last night. Hell—don't tell anyone we was even there at all last night. Keep your mouth shut. Promise me."

There's a silence.

"Lissa, what happened last night after Becka and me left? You tell me."

So I tell her everything, and Cindy keeps saying, "Oh, my Lord," over and over, which is getting on my nerves real bad, so I tell her that unless she can come up with something constructive to say, to just shut up. She's quiet for a minute.

"Lissa, the police are surely gonna be talking with people that were at the bar last night. Did anybody see you with Brian?"

"Of course they did. I mean, while we were in the bar, they did. I don't know about out in the parking lot. I wasn't really paying attention. We were just sitting in the bus talking for a few minutes till everybody cleared out."

"Well, somebody's gonna tell them and they're gonna know you were with him and they'll be coming to you asking questions."

I know she's right, and my stomach does a flip.

"You better have you a good alibi ready," she says.

"Alibi? I didn't kill him, Cindy. He was alive when I left—I swear he was. Stinking drunk, but alive. You believe me, don't you? Cindy?"

"Uh—well, sure I do, Lissa, but—"

"Just promise me you'll keep your mouth shut about what I told you."

"Okay, I promise. But if they ask me, I'll have to at least tell them I was there. Becka too. You know she ain't no good at lying."

"All right. I gotta go to work for awhile this afternoon. Let me know if you hear anything else, okay?"

"All right, Lissa. Look, I gotta go now. I'll call you later."

I'm pulling on some jeans and a blouse when Gabe rolls his chair into the bedroom. He doesn't look at all happy with me. "Where were you last night, Lissa? And don't tell me you were at the Diner, because it doesn't stay open until any three a.m." He's paler than usual, and he's got dark circles around his eyes, like he didn't sleep very much.

Originally, I had an elaborate story planned involving a breakdown with the bus and a heater hose, but I figure he's probably gonna find out where I was anyway, so I go on and tell him we was at Riverview Bar. "The Diner was dead, Gabe. Cindy wanted a beer."

"Well, that's one fine place for a wife and mother of two small children to be going, isn't it?"

I look at him, hands on my hips. "As a matter of fact, it's the *perfect* place for a wife and mother of two small children to go. I told you I had to get out."

Gabe punches the arm of his chair. "So what am I supposed to think, when you're out until three o'clock in the morning, Lissa? *Huh? What?*"

"Well, I guess you go ahead and think whatever the hell it is you want, 'cause you will anyway, ain't that right, Gabe?"

He lifts his finger and has his mouth poised to say something else, but Hailey creeps in and stands by the door, eyes bugging out of her head, chewing on her finger. "Mama? Bug got sick on the kitchen floor," she says. I can barely hear her.

Gabe twirls the chair around and rolls it into the kitchen. "What'd you eat, Bug?" I hear him say. "God, Bug, what'd you get into?"

I walk into the kitchen and Bug is in a little heap on the floor next to a puddle of puke, holding his stomach and crying softly. I bend down and pick him up. He's pale and there are white crystals all over his mouth.

"Daddy, my tummy hoots," he says.

Gabe's eyes get big and panicky. "He got into some kind of poison; I *know* it. Get an ambulance on the phone, quick."

Hailey is standing behind the table wringing her hands, and she starts to cry.

I brush at the white stuff on Bug's face, look down at the kitchen stool, and see a spoon and the sugar bowl—empty—setting on it.

"It ain't poison, it's sugar," I tell him. "It ain't gonna hurt him none, but he's gonna have a stomachache for a while. Hailey, go on in your room and play with your doll or something. Everybody calm down, for God's sake. *Shit.*"

I lay Bug face down on the sofa and let him groan, and I clean up the puke and the sugar. "You could have fed him, you know," I tell Gabe.

"I fed him toast and jelly three hours ago, while you were still lying in bed," he says, and since he can't stomp around or nothing, he goes into the living room and turns up the TV

I'm wiping off the stool with a dishcloth, cartoons blaring, and Bug is still whining, his face in the cushions. *They think they got problems,* I'm thinking. *They don't know what real troubles are till they're waiting for the police to come and take them away.*

And then I'm hearing a knocking on the trailer door—that tin-can kind of knock—and my heart stops.

3

Willie

Saturday, May 5, 1973

Fishing around in a dumpster this morning, I've found myself a ten-dollar bill. Dug it up out of a ripped Hardee's bag full of soggy fries and crumpled paper. After I first found the bag, I was giving consideration to eating the fries when I heard something jingling down in the bottom of that dark and greasy bag, so I pulled the paper out and uncovered two pennies and a folded-up bill among the fries. I had to unfold the bill and hold it up in front of my good eye to make sure I was seeing right, 'cause the poor light in the alley can play tricks on my old eyes. But here it is—a bona fide ten-dollar bill, Alexander Hamilton's mug smiling up at me, sure enough.

There was a time, long ago, when I first hit the streets, I was too proud to pick up a penny, even if I was sick hungry. The first time I found a twenty, I hadn't eaten anything in four days, not a scrap. I'd been praying to God I could have something to eat. I told Him it didn't have to be my papa's fried chicken—I didn't expect that; even an old, stale piece of bread would do. I walked around town 'cause I didn't know what else to do, and I found the twenty lying right outside the Piggly Wiggly, like somebody had their arms too full of grocery bags and dropped it in the parking lot.

I bent over and picked it up, and first thing I done, I marched right in the store and handed it to the manager standing up in his little glassed-in room over in the corner, and told him where I found it. He took it from me and nodded, and said, "Well, I'll take care of it." I nodded and walked away, and as I walked out of the store I turned around and saw him stuffing that bill right down into his own wallet.

When I got outside, I plunked down right on the curb and thunk hard about that, the walls of my stomach all caved in and just a-rubbing away on theirselves, 'cause they ain't got nothing else to do. Then it occurred to me I had been praying for something to eat and God had answered by sending me that twenty, but I was just too stupid to realize it. That were a long time ago.

To an old bum like me, this ten dollars might as well be a *hundred* dollars, 'cause I ain't got nothing, unless you call an old refrigerator box that I sleep in something. It's big enough to crawl inside and still have a little leg room, so I call it home. At one time I kept it under an overhang up behind Al's Appliance Store—boarded up for three years now, ever since Al died—till one windy night back in March, aliens nearly destroyed the box, with me still inside.

One chilly night I was lying there inside the box, listening to the wind outside and the rumbling of thunder and minding my own business, just about to fall asleep, and them creatures come around and started pounding on the outside of the box with some kind of bat. I scootched up into one corner of the box, afraid to even yell out in case they got their laser guns. Then they started laughing and rocking it back and forth like they're gonna tip it over, yelling about are there any drunks inside and such as that. By the noise they made, I judged there to be about four or five of them.

It's a known fact that an alien will try to disguise hisself as one of us so he can walk around on this earth with no trouble. At this particular instance, a group of them was trying to pass as a bunch of punk kids, but they didn't fool me. One of them said, "We got us a tramp-in-the-box; let's see if we can pop the top." Then they started singing "Pop Goes the Weasel," and when they got to the end where it says *POP*, they turned the whole thing over and I come spilling out, along with my collection of shells and my *Life* magazine and the crumpled newspapers I use to keep myself warm.

They all whooped it up laughing, 'cause the sight of me lying on the ground all flustered-like was riotous funny to them. And to make matters worse, a light, cold rain started falling.

After a minute or so, two of them hauled me up by my clothes so I was standing up in the middle of them, and one of them—he got long, stringy hair and yellow teeth, reminded me of a rat—took out his knife.

"Slice him up good, man," another one said.

I held out my hands and said, "I ain't done nothing to you, now," and that gave them aliens another good chuckle. I wonder why he didn't just take out his ray gun instead of that blade and be done with it, but I guess they was into the sport of it. So he started moving that knife around and circling around me, and all I could think to do was put up my two fists like I'm gonna spar with him, just like I used to do with my big brother Luke.

The alien rat kid grinned real big, showing his yellow teeth, and jabbed at me with that blade, slicing my left hand—it felt like a sharp sting. So I took the chance and threw a right hook at him while he was off balance, and I caught him on the jaw—not solid, but enough to snap it shut and make him bite his tongue hard.

One of his buddies laughed, if that's what you could call it—a high, frenzied howl coming out of his mouth—and the alien drew air in through his teeth, making a sound like a snake, and screwed his face all up into such a mask of rage as I ain't never before seen. He thrust that knife backhanded this time, and caught my right arm below the elbow. I saw a trickle of blood come out the corner of his mouth. I punched at him with my left fist, but he was too fast this time and dodged out of the way. My heart was a-pounding hard in my chest. He was grinning again, and eyeing me with such hate. I swung again, but one of his friends went and kicked my legs out from under me and I went down on my knees, looking down into a puddle of blood. I wondered whose it was, till I saw it dripping down from both of my own hands.

The alien rat kid started circling around me again, saying, "You better go on and pray while you're down there, old man, 'cause you're gonna—"

Right at that moment a siren come blaring from over on Oak Street, heading our way fast. Them aliens didn't wait to see what it might be, they just ran out of there in a panic, but not before that rat alien pointed a finger at me, and I saw blood foaming through his clenched teeth when he said, "You're *dead*, man." Then he was gone.

Turned out that siren belonged to a fire truck headed out of town. Hadn't been for that, there's no telling what else they would've done. I just collapsed on the ground where I was and took stock of my cuts. The one on my hand weren't too bad. I should've had stitches on the one below my elbow, but if a man like me walks into the emergency room with a wound like that, they's gonna call the police right away. Plus, I don't have no way to pay for it. So I poured a little of my arthritis medicine on the cuts and wrapped them up tight with some old rags, and hoped for the best. I poured a little of that medicine down my throat, too, so it could work from the inside out.

I gathered up my stuff the best I could, although the magazine and newspapers were blowing around and got soaked through. I was so sore and shook so bad I couldn't go to sleep; I was afraid they might come back and finish the job, so I crouched inside my box and shivered the night through, just thankful to be in one piece. Even though He's mostly forgotten me, I think the Lord was looking down on me that night.

After that I moved my box closer into town, over in an alley on Third between the pawnshop and the auto parts store. Nobody ever goes in that alley except me; there ain't any reason to. So I slid the box up against the brick wall and I made some what you'd call modifications to it, too—camouflaging it with all manner of things I found around town, like a section of an old tin roof, a tire, and a torn up tarp. Anybody goes into that dark old alley, they won't even know that box is there now. Another plus is that the piece of tin will break up the signal the aliens have directed on me, so they can't find me.

I did manage to salvage my collection of shells from the alien attack. They ain't as eye-catching as they was when I first spied them on the beach, all shiny and washed in rainbow colors like you see in little oil puddles on the street, but they's still appealing. If I walk on the beach it's at the first light of day, before much of anybody else is out. You go down there the morning after a storm, that's when you find the best shells washed up during the night. The ones that are whole are chock full of good luck, don't you know, 'cause they made it through all them breakers without getting broke. I pick them up off the sand and bring them back and hang them up from the ceiling inside the box by poking little holes in it with a bent up hanger and then tying them with bits of string. That way I can get the good out of them while I sleep.

I got me a new *Life* I fished out of a dumpster behind the doctor's office—a more recent issue. I also have a thick piece of candle, some matches from the café over on Pine, and one half of a set of binoculars I dug out of the sand down at the beach, which comes in awful handy for scoping out the night heavens for UFOs. Sometimes during tourist season you can find the darndest things.

I have me a real blanket someone dropped off the back of a moving truck two weeks ago, one of those quilted kinds. It's small but in pretty good shape, so I use it to sleep on. I don't really need a lot of newspapers anymore since the nights are warmer, but I have a reserve stack of them tied up with string there in the alley beside the box, under the tarp to keep them dry. So you see, although I have *nothing*, I at least have enough of it to keep me alive. And to give myself the illusion that it's *something*, I have dubbed the box my Palace.

I lie low during the day, when folks are moving about around town, and especially during the summer when the tourist season brings throngs of them and their cars and boats and RVs. If anyone sees me they'll know I'm a bum with my ragged clothes and holey shoes and matted hair—or they'll say I'm a hippie, but I'm not. A hippie *wants* to be this way.

I seen lots of hippies passing through here; most of the time they don't cause no trouble. Unless they're in a big group, they stay low, like me.

One summer night it was so hot and humid I couldn't breathe, much less sleep, so I walked down to the beach and searched around and found me a place along a little dune to stretch out so I could feel the salt breeze coming off the ocean, but at the same time I couldn't be seen. I was lying there resting and this tall, nice-looking kid with shoulder-length hair come walking down the beach and he must have got the same idea, 'cause he come over and stood looking down at me, his hair blowing in the breeze. He didn't look like your regular hippie type, just some kid passing through; maybe got into some drugs.

"Can I crash here, man?" he asked me.

I figured he had as much right to sleep there as I did, so I said, "All right."

He didn't say another word, just sat down a few feet away and took a bag of potato chips out of his poncho and started munching on them. After he been a-munching and crunching for a while, he held the bag out to me, and I took me a few, to be polite. He didn't say nothing; he just finished that whole bag off and lay down and went right to sleep. I dozed off too, but not for long, 'cause first thing I knew, that hippie's jostling me awake. I sat up, wondering what he wanted. He was sitting there swatting at his head like he had flies buzzing around him or something.

"Could you do me a favor, man?" he said to me.

"What is it?" I asked him.

"Could you tell me if my head is on fire?"

I looked at him to see if he was joking, but he kept swatting at hisself and his eyes were bugging out like a scared kid. I shook my head. "No, it ain't," I told him. "Your head is just fine."

He patted his head all over and took down his hands and stared at them, then he grinned at me, real grateful-like. "Thanks, man," he said, and laid hisself down again. I didn't hear a peep out of him the rest of the night. In the morning, he was gone when I woke up. But there was a unopened bag of chips there in the sand, right beside me.

Once I found a broken fishing knife and sawed my fuzzy hair off shorter, but it grew back worse than ever. There's a water spigot outside the motel down at the beach, and sometimes I sneak down there and clean myself up the best I can, but I have to be careful or someone will call the police. If they pick me up it's just a big hassle to go through, 'cause nobody knows what to do with me—they know it and I know it. So they pretty much leave me be, unless they get that call.

Although I'm always pretty much on my own, I got me a pet dog. He's a little old thing, dirty white with a black mask and ears—about as scraggly as I am and missing his right front leg, so that he limps when he walks. Only when he walks, though. He can run something fierce on his three legs when he wants to. Just goes to prove, you don't have to be whole to get by. I guess there's a lot of us in the world got a piece missing, though it don't necessarily show.

First time I saw him was a few days after the alien attack. He was scrounging around on the ground at the dumpster near the restaurant where I usually look for the best scraps, ribs poking through his skin, so I figured the little mutt was hungry like me. He was skittish and wouldn't let me near him, and I wondered if he'd been plagued by them aliens hisself. I dug through the mess and found a good-sized steak bone with a little bit of dried meat still on it, and held it out for him until he was finally brave enough to come to me. He growled and jerked it out of my hand, and ran off on his three legs with it. I figured I wouldn't see him again after that.

But there he was the next morning, sticking his head around the corner of the Palace and peeking in at me, grease still shiny on his whiskers and him still licking his chops. He must've worked on that bone all night long. When I looked up and seen that little fella's face poking into the Palace like that, it gave me such a thrill to see him again, I threw back my head and had me a good belly laugh. Near scared us both to death. It'd been so long since I heard myself laugh, for a second I had to turn around to see who was making all that noise. Lord, it felt good.

I ain't never heard him bark. When he first started coming around, there was times he weren't around for days, and then I'd look up and see him standing there, head tilted, eyeballing me to see what I was up to. He hardly made no noise at all, appearing and disappearing when you least expected it, so I call him "Goblin." You could also take that as "Gobblin'," 'cause that's what he do to them delicacies I throw at his feet.

I guess he got used to being around me, 'cause now he stays right by my side, night and day, like we was attached at the hip. He climbs right on into the Palace at night and settles hisself down in the corner by my feet like he's paying rent. He don't let me touch him much, though—he's still skittish as they come. You see anybody that jumpy, it's a fact they been mistreated. It ain't a easy way to live, the way he and I do, but it's all we got.

But now I have myself a ten-dollar bill and I wad up that greasy hamburger bag and pitch it back in the trash. No cold, limp, old fries for me; uh-uh—today I eat big. Like I said, mostly I lay low, but if ever I get me some money, I can move around like as if I'm Somebody, almost.

First I take my money over to the ABC store and purchase a bottle of arthritis medicine, which I been needing on account of using it up on my knife cuts. After the alien attack, them cuts hurt like almighty hell for awhile, and me thinking they might be infected, but I just kept pouring that medicine on them and they finally decided to calm down—now the edges of them ain't got that angry look to them.

I take and deposit the bottle of medicine safely at the Palace, and head straight on over to the café, where I buy myself a piece of homemade sweet potato pie, smiling big as you please, Goblin waiting for me right outside the door. But they hurry me right out again directly—after taking the money. Apparently I ain't so good for business. I swear they didn't give me enough change, but when I try to go back and explain, they just tell me I don't know how to count. There ain't no use to go making a big fuss. So I carry my little paper bag with the pie in it home to the Palace, Goblin and me crawl inside, and as I eat it and break off a chunk for Goblin—which he vacuums up like it's a dust bunny—I thank the Lord to be so blessed.

The pie surely stirs up memories of home. My mama used to make sweet potato pie. Lord, was it *awful*. She was such a sweet little old God-fearing woman, but anything she whipped up in the kitchen tasted like it was spawned by the devil himself. The harder she tried, the worse it got. Got so bad, we couldn't even trick the dog into eating it. But there was seven of us kids to feed and we had to eat something, so Papa eventually took over the cooking.

At first his buddies down at the gas station used to ride him something awful about taking up woman's work. Then one day Big Andy happened by when we all was eating some chicken Papa'd fried up for supper after church, so Mama got up and set down a extra place for him at the table. All us kids watched as Big Andy took that first bite, and his eyes got all big. He scarfed down all the chicken on his plate and all the mashed potatoes and gravy and greens and asked for more.

I never heard so much bragging as Big Andy did over Papa's cooking. He showed up the next Sunday, too, and brought a friend. Next thing you know, we had so many folks coming to supper on Sunday evenings after church, I didn't know who half of them was—white folks, too. And I still don't know how he did it, but Papa always had enough for everyone. Nobody ever got up from that table hungry.

Like I said, there was seven of us kids, me being the youngest, and I guess Mama got tired of naming her children after folks from the Bible—like Luke and Mary and Joshua and Moses and Joseph and Sarah—'cause the same year I came along, which was nineteen and twenty-eight, she'd caught a gander at the first animated film that could talk, *Steamboat Willie*, and that's how I came to be named after a mouse, instead. Whenever she caught anybody teasing me about it, Mama would tell them to hush and that I was her "special child" who was destined to go far in this world.

We kids used to get into all kinds of fun. There was such a big range atween the eldest—Mary—and me, till she thought she was my mama, and she taught me to read before I was even in first grade. She used to fuss something *awful* about my bad grammar, but I never got it quite right, like they was some kind of block in my head. Anyway, I told her I couldn't see much use to using fancy words when Papa didn't, and I always thought of him as a successful man although he didn't make a whole lot of money, and she had to agree with that. Lord knows she tried her best with me, though, teaching me poetry and even lines from Shakespeare whenever she took a notion. Then she married a doctor and left home to start her own family.

I learned how to spar some from my brother Luke, who wanted to be a great heavyweight boxer like Joe Louis more than anything in the world. Somehow or other, though, he ended up teaching the fifth grade at Lincoln J. Bailey Elementary School.

Me, I dreamed of being a major-league baseball player like Jackie Robinson. I turned nine the year he signed up with the Brooklyn Dodgers, and I got me a brand new baseball mitt for my birthday. We kids—the ones of us still living at home—would get us a neighborhood game going in the vacant lot beside the drugstore almost every Saturday, come rain or shine, using whatever we could find for bases. None of us much cared whether we won or lost. We just loved playing.

There was this little girl in my seventh grade English class called Iris. She had pretty eyes—big, like a deer's eyes—and skin the color of honey. She sat one row up ahead of me, and I'd sit there every day moonin' over her till I was half sick. She wouldn't have nothing to do with me, though. If we was walking down the hall, I'd catch up to her and I'd try to carry her books, but she'd just shift them over to her other arm and keep on walking. I figured she must be interested in somebody else, so eventually I give up, although I still couldn't help but stare at her in class.

One morning I woke up late and ran all the way to school, knowing I'd done already missed the bell, and as I was about to run up the steps there she was, Iris, sitting all huddled on the bottom step, crying like she ain't never gonna stop. So I sat down next to her and let her cry for awhile, and then I asked her what's wrong.

She looked up at me, those big doe eyes still spilling over, and I give her my handkerchief. "I ain't never going home again," she said.

"Why not?" I asked her, and she shook her head and covered up her face. "My mama, she always bringing home men," she said. "Sometimes, they wanna come in my room and bother me."

I had a notion as to what she meant by that, so I said, "Oh."

"I ain't gonna stand for it no more. This last time? That man she brought home smelling like old whisky? After Mama asleep, late last night, he come creeping into my room, just like I knowed he would. What he didn't know was, I had my lunchbox hid under the covers with me. I waited till he was standing up next to my bed, and I swung that box out and slammed it into his balls. He just crumpled up on the floor and his eyes rolled back in his head—I thought I'd killed him. He lay there for a long time, hardly moving and making little high sounds in his throat like a squeaky door, till finally he half-crawled to the back door and let hisself out.

"This morning Mama gets up and she's looking for him, yelling, 'Henry, *where you at?*' And she gets all anxious when she figures out he ain't there. She comes around asking me do I know where he is, and I tell her, 'I don't know and I don't care.' Then she gets mad and slaps *me*."

I didn't know what to say, so I put my arm around her shoulder and stared at the ground.

"She shouldn't ought to get mad at *me*," she said, and started sobbing again.

I sat there with her for awhile, till she got quiet. She held out my handkerchief, all soaked through. "That's okay, Iris," I told her. "You go on and keep it, case you want it again later." And she broke into a little smile. After that Iris let me carry her books, but she never talked about them men or her mama no more.

I took her to a dance at the school that spring. Papa drove me to her house to pick her up, and she come to the door smiling, all decked out in a dress the color of sea green, the fancy kind that's got them full petticoats under it and rustles when she walks. She looked so fine I had to steady my hand in order to pin the carnation on her. All that evening with her on my arm, it was like I was walking on a cloud.

That summer, when school let out, she and her mama moved away. Oh, I had other girl friends after that, don't you know. But Iris is the one took my heart with her when she left.

One by one my brothers and sisters grew up and left home to be all manner of successful people. But came my turn to go off to college, something happened. My thinking started getting fuzzy now and then, like my head was stuffed full of quilt batting. Sometimes I would hear voices telling me what to do, but nobody else could hear them. When one of them voices told me to walk out in front of a bus, I knew something was bad wrong. Papa took me to some doctors and they gave me some pills to make the voices go away, and I took them for awhile. But they made me feel like a zombie walking around, so I quit. Soon them voices came back and explained how them doctors were really demons trying to kill me with them pills—demons are worse than aliens, don't you know. Well, you keep hearing something over and over again, after a while you start to believe it.

They was one voice in particular, wanted to be in charge. I could tell that right away, the first time I heard him. He said his name was Jake, and that he was older than dirt. He said he knew just about everything there was to know and if I followed his directions, I would get to be falling-down rich someday, wearing fine clothes and driving a fine, shiny car and living in a fine house and having to beat the women off me with a stick. I just laughed at that, but he had a way of making you listen even if you didn't want to, I swear he did. There were others, but he was the worst.

Since I couldn't go to college after all on account of my sickness, I got the notion I could learn to cook from Papa and open me up a restaurant someday. Papa liked the idea too, and so I started learning right away, hanging around in the kitchen whenever he was there and helping out however I could. Soon I found out I really liked to cook, and Mama even said I had a calling for it.

Then one evening I was sitting at the kitchen table peeling potatoes and Jake come in the room telling me to take the knife I was using and stick Papa in the neck with it. Just like that, he ordered me to do it—said if I'm a real man I would—and if I don't, something really bad gonna happen to me one day. *He'd see to it*, he said, no matter how long it took.

My papa is the kind of man, never raised a hand to nobody—he just as soon cut it off as do harm. I just stared at the knife in my hand, the edge of it all keen and sharp in order to slice through them potatoes real easy, my mouth hanging open, till Papa said, "Boy, what's the matter with you?"

I didn't answer him. I just let the knife slip out of my hand, got up from the table, and walked out that very day, not bothering to say goodbye or pack any clothes or tell anybody where I was going, 'cause I didn't know myself.

I don't know how many years I spent running from demons. I call them my "lost years," 'cause I can't remember a whole lot about them, only that it was like I was wandering around in a dark, dark place—like a bad dream I couldn't rouse myself out of. I lost my youth, I lost my self-respect, I lost track of everything that was normal and decent in this life, including my own family. However it was I came to be here in this place, this town, it was then I stopped running. I guess 'cause being here next to the great Atlantic, I ran out of places to go.

My sister Mary somehow managed to find me once, and tried to take me back with her, but I just couldn't go home and face Mama. I was supposed to be her special child, after all. Then a couple years later, one cold winter day, she found me again. She told me Mama and Papa had both passed, one right after the other. "You might as well come on home with me now, Willie," she said to me.

Mary was already a grandmother taking care of two grandbabies herself. I told her I was too old to start over. "You go on and live your life," I told her. "I'll be all right."

She stuffed a little money into my hand and hugged me tight for a moment, her face all sad. "I love you, Willie," she told me, the snow falling down quiet around her like goose down. And then she walked away, boots crunching in the snow, her familiar shape fading into the cold, wet fog hanging over the street.

When she was gone I was still staring down at the place where she'd been standing, the snow filling in her footprints till they was hard to see. "I love you too, big sister," I said then. I ain't never seen her again.

But there's one curious thing. For some reason I'm not privy to, most of them voices have faded away these last some-odd years, and took the demons with them. Now it's mainly aliens want to get me, but I know how to handle them. You just gotta keep one step ahead of 'em—that's the secret.

I feel pretty good now. The sweet potato pie's down in my stomach so it got something to work on for awhile, and I take me a good slug of my medicine. The low grumble of thunder tells me there's a storm gathering itself together somewhere out there over the ocean. I take another swallow from the bottle and it goes down nice and warm, and after a while I feel like taking me a nap. So I stretch out on my blanket, my eyelids falling heavy, like they got weights on them.

I must have fell asleep for awhile, 'cause all of a sudden I see this white light shining right through my closed eyelids, it's so bright. My eyes pop open wide. The inside of the Palace is all lit up, too. Goblin is already sitting up in his corner, his head a-leaning to one side and then the other.

First thing that pops into my mind is, them aliens come back in their spacecraft to get me, so I grab up my medicine bottle by the neck and draw myself into one corner of the box, watching that white light streaming in through every tiny hole in that box there is—through the little holes in the ceiling for the strings that got the seashells hanging on them, and especially through the door, which is only just a rag I got hanging over the cutout—and I tell myself I ain't going without a good fight. I listen hard, but I can't hear nothing but a low rumble of thunder and the pattering of rain falling outside, and I can smell the musty odor of damp mold from the alley.

That light streams in and I sit there all crouched up for what seems a long time, but in reality probably only a minute or so. Finally that beam fades away slow, till the Palace is dark again, the only faint light there is, coming through the rag door. I still can't hear nothing, so I begin to get the notion I should peek out and see if there's anything out there for myself, 'cause I can't just keep hunched up here holding up that bottle forever. I'm turning my head from one side to the other in order to hone in on the least little sound, and I lean forward, then crawl toward the rag door that's fluttering a bit in the breeze.

I hold my breath and grab that rag, and then I rip it aside.

4

Sera

Saturday, May 5, 1973

10:15 a.m.

One moment I am cradled in an ethereal light, the next it is as though a switch is flipped, plunging me into inky blackness. Vision returns to my open eyes in little pinpoints, starting at the outer edges and moving inward until I can focus on my new surroundings. Only then do I realize I have come to the end of my journey.

With the return of my sight, there's a sudden rush upon all of my senses—the fresh smell of ozone in rainwashed air laced with an underlying odor of mold and old things; the flash of light across a dark gray sky, chased by a peal of thunder. Cold drops of rain patter against my shoulders and a gust of wind raises goose bumps on my exposed skin.

I'm standing half in and half out of a narrow space between two buildings—a small alley. Until I get my bearings, I prefer to remain unseen, so I duck into the passage as the sky opens up and the rain falls in torrents. Frantically I look around, seeing only a jumble of old junk: a wavy sheet of metal propped against a ragged old box, a flapping sheet of plastic thrown haphazardly over it.

Crouching down on my toes, I lift up part of the plastic sheet to cover my head, uncovering a cloth on the side of the box that is flapping gently in the breeze, as though it's covering up a hole. The rain is soaking me; I consider crawling inside, maybe finding shelter, but I wonder if some sort of animal may be inside. My teeth are beginning to chatter. Holding my breath, I fling back the cloth.

The world lights up with a flash of lightning and there, framed in the hole, are two white-rimmed eyes bulging in a black face, its mouth gaping open in a silent scream.

Thunder crashes as I fall back on my heels; a shriek escapes my lungs and pierces my own ears as I scramble to pick myself up, only to catch my foot in a rip in the plastic sheet. I trip, tumbling headfirst into the brick wall and falling down beside the box again. Dizzy, I hold my forehead, my heart racing, and stare at the cloth, which now covers the hole again.

Slowly the cloth is drawn partially aside, revealing the face in the shadows.

It's only a man. He appears as bewildered as I. We stare at one another until the man moves his lips a little, as though swearing under his breath. Then he says, "You an alien?"

Hysteria wells up in my throat, but I swallow hard and somehow manage to gain control. Although I don't understand the nature of the man's question, I sense by his inflection that it's best I say no. "No."

Relief spreads over his dark features and the glaze goes out of his eyes. It's like he's awakening from sleep. "You're bleeding," he says, frowning. He points to my head.

I drop my hand from my forehead, and see blood on my fingers. I still feel dazed. I don't know what to say.

The man gently pulls the curtain all the way back. "Child, you better come on in out of that rain, now."

I'm wary; I shake my head, blinking at the rain-diluted blood running down into my eyes.

He nods. "You do what you want, but I ain't gonna hurt you, and you ain't getting any drier out there. If you don't come in here, you at least better go find yourself someplace to get out of this storm. You gonna catch your death."

I consider what he has said, and I decide, against my better judgment, to trust the very first person I have seen in the year 1973. As I crawl through the opening in the box, it occurs to me that this man is already long gone, turned to dust, by the year I was born. Yet here we are, face to face. The thought is overwhelming.

It is so dim inside that I can barely make anything out, but my eyes slowly become accustomed. The man has drawn his legs up, bunching himself up in a corner to make room for me. I am surprised to see we aren't alone; a small dog stares at me from the corner next to him. The little dog's head is tilted, one of his floppy ears standing almost straight up, giving him a comical look. There is not enough clearance to sit up straight, so I lean to the side on one elbow.

The man searches through a pile of rags beside him and holds one out to me. "This rag's part of a old towel," he says. "Reckon it's clean enough, you can dry yourself off with it, if you want."

"Thank you." I accept the rag and begin doing just that. After I've dried myself off as best I can, I wrap the damp towel around my wet hair so it won't drip onto the floor of the box.

Watching the ease with which he contorts himself to find this and that, I am beginning to understand that the man lives here—this is his home. He hands me another rag. "You better hold this one to your head," he says.

My forehead is still bleeding, where it hit the brick wall. "I tripped and fell," I explain, pressing the cloth to my head.

"You just hold that on there and it'll stop, soon enough."

The man touches the dog's head lightly and it lies down again, still looking at me.

Now I can see well enough to notice small objects hanging by strings from the top of the box. "What are these?" I ask.

"They my good luck charms. I found each and every one of them myself, so I know they full of good luck. The ones you sitting under? The luck's falling down from them right onto your head, as we speak."

I touch one of them and recognize its smooth, scalloped shape. "There's a beach close by, then?"

He frowns. "Right down the street and a couple of blocks over."

I catch my breath. I have never been this close to the sea. Now I'm aware of the pounding of the surf. Although it is muffled, it's audible even over the racket from the rain.

The man and his dog are regarding me closely from their little huddle.

"My name is Sera."

"Sera," he says, as if savoring a new name. "You can call me Willie, and this here's Goblin."

"Thank you, Willie, for letting me stay inside here for a while."

"Ain't no reason to mention it," he says. Then he laughs, a rich, hearty sound within the cardboard walls. Goblin begins to pant, giving him the illusion of laughing, too. "You give me quite a start, Sera, you surely did."

"I'm sorry. I didn't know anyone was here."

The man—Willie—stops laughing, his brow crinkling into a frown. It frightens me a little. "You ain't from around here, I know it. Fact is, you come in on a bright, white laser beam, ain't that right?"

I'm startled that he would know this, and I remember my instructions not to disclose the nature of my visit. "It must have been a flash of lightning you saw," I say, "just before."

He shakes his head. "I know a flash of lightning, child. But I seen a lot of strange things in my life, too. And I know a UFO when I see it. You may not be exactly like them aliens that attacked me, but I know you ain't from this world, neither, so don't try to tell me different. *You can't fool old Willie.*"

I think about what he has said, my forehead burning from the knock it has taken. I have only been here for a few minutes, and already I've managed to reveal myself, although he is wrong about my being an alien. "What the hell." I dig into the leather bag at my waist and bring out a first aid kit, flipping open the small metal box. "I'm not an alien. I've traveled here from the future."

"Oh." He gives an understanding nod. "One of *them.*"

I unroll the bandage, a small square of soft, rubbery mesh, and place it on my forehead, pressing it gently to the cut. As it warms, the bandage fuses to the open wound, sealing it shut. Then it becomes as smooth as my own skin. I pull the excess mesh off my forehead, and the cut is gone.

"Lord, if I hadn't seen it with my own eyes, I'd never believe it," he says.

I snap the box shut and put it back into my bag, squinting at him. "I thought you just said you'd seen a lot of strange things."

He raises an eyebrow and thinks for a moment. "Well, you're right about that, it's a fact." He points at my forehead. "Will you tell me how that thing works?"

I shrug. "I don't know how, it just does."

"Now, how can you go and use it and not know how it works?"

"Do *you* know how everything works around here?"

"Well, no; I can't say that I do," he admits.

We sit listening to the rain for awhile. An occasional car passes on the waterlogged street outside, its tires pushing through the water with a loud swoosh. I glance at Willie. He looks tired and there are deep circles under his eyes. "Why do you live here, Willie?"

He understands that I mean *here*, inside the box. It's not a tactful question, but he seems like a man who appreciates directness. "Sometimes I look around me and ask myself that very question: *why?* So far I ain't come upon a satisfying answer. But I can tell you *how* I come to be here, if you want to hear it."

I shift my cramped position into a more comfortable one. "I'd like that very much."

So Willie tells me his story while the rain falls outside. As he speaks, I watch as a range of emotions wash over his tired face, and observe the sentient sparkle that plays in the deep wells of his eyes. I'm shocked to learn he is only forty-five years old. His once dark hair and beard are splotched with patches of white. The lines of his face are deep furrows, and at least two of his teeth are missing. He looks seventy, perhaps older. I find myself touched by his self-effacement, drawn by his earnestness. And even as he tells me he is insane, I find him to be more rational than anyone I have ever known. Perhaps it's his world that is insane.

When Willie is through, he lets out a long sigh and tries to stretch out his legs. "You got anything in that little bag for arthritis?"

I smile and shake my head. "There is no arthritis where I come from. And these are only for minor cuts and scratches, I'm afraid."

He picks up the bottle beside him and unscrews its cap. "That's all right," he says, chuckling. "I got my own magic. Now it's *your* turn, Miss Sera."

"What do you mean?"

"Well, I told you about myself, now you tell me about you. I'd be interested to hear it, if you wouldn't mind telling me."

There's nowhere to go until the storm passes, and somehow I feel I owe him as much. So I tell Willie about the world I live in, a world even more alien to him than his own. I talk about the great city, my apartment, the Wheel, and the Cosmos Coffee Shop where I work. I even tell him about Father and about Dr. Moore and Dr. Weiss.

I explain about EyeCom and energy signatures, and then I tell him why I'm here. As I describe all these things to him, Willie's dark eyes reflect the wonder of them, and I am aware of how it all must sound to him. And seeing it through his eyes like that makes me wonder at all of it a little, too. He listens intently, slack-jawed and wide-eyed, like a child, his bottle forgotten.

He is silent for a time.

"So you and I come from the same planet, only a different time."

"That's right. I know it sounds impossible..."

"Ain't nobody can make up a story like that. They got any black folks like me?"

"Of course. But I've never seen anyone with skin as dark as yours." I think of how people in my time wash themselves in color, and I know they would think his skin beautiful, as though it were a fresh palette filled with new possibilities.

He leans his head back against the cardboard wall. "Now, I got to ask you this—what about war? You-all got war up in the future? 'Cause it seems like we always got one or two bad ones always going on here. Always worrying about the bomb, too." I think of the wars fought since his time, and it is difficult to tell him the whole truth. "There will always be war, I think. The ones in my time are not as bloody. There are few humans on the battlefield, and more machines. But the technology is such that we have to be very careful. Your bomb is nothing, Willie, compared with what we have." I'm unable to look at his face when I tell him this.

"Well," he says. "Least it's good to know we'll still be running around on this old earth a while longer."

"There's less crime," I say, trying to relay something happy. "With EyeCom, everyone eventually gets caught. So only fools try anything."

Willie laughs once again, his eyes crinkling. "Just goes to prove they ain't never gonna be a shortage of fools."

He looks at me, his eyelids heavy. "If you from the future, Miss Sera, and you know some about the folks living right here and now, do you know when it is I'm gonna die?"

"I don't. But you wouldn't really want to know that anyway, would you?"

He carefully considers this. "I been in the dark about things so long now, I don't think the knowing would be so bad." He closes his eyes.

Before long his jaw goes slack, his grip on the bottle loosens. I gently slide the bottle from under his hand and hold it up to my nose, then draw it quickly away. I screw the cap back onto it and set it down carefully beside him where he can find it when he wakes.

Goblin lies with his head on his one front paw, still watching me. "Take care of Willie," I whisper to him, and his tail thumps once.

I move the cloth flap aside; the rain has mostly stopped. Steam rises from the street in thin, feathery wisps, and the gray sky is brightening through the haze. A boy pedals by on his bicycle, and a car sizzles past over still-wet pavement. I think it's time for me to go.

According to my communicator band—disguised as a Mickey Mouse watch—I've only a short distance to walk to find my destination. I can hear the persistent pounding of the surf growing clearer as I walk down one block and then another. The clouds part and the first rays of sunlight after the storm bathe the world in a warm, yellow glow. Steam still rises from the streets. Birds have begun to stir, flapping in little puddles and singing from trees. People venture outside and move about, too.

This year, 1973, is not just a time, but also a place. I am here in a place where Sera does not exist. Here I have no past, no home. There is nothing at all to spark the slightest memory because I have none.

I nod and smile at a woman getting the mail from her mailbox at her door. She smiles back at me. To her I am just a woman walking down Oak Street, but in reality I am only a shadow of things to come—an illusion. And yet I *am* real, and they are not. My thoughts tie themselves into knots, endless loops of nonsense. No one on this earth knows me, just as I do not know them, except for Willie. I think about him, sound asleep in his box home. He seems very real. What a curious introduction I have had to this place.

The ocean is very near now, although rows of trailers block it from view. If I were to stay on the road I am on, I'm certain it would lead me down to the water. Instead I turn into the park's sandy main drive and walk along inspecting the names on the mailboxes. Some of them are in bad shape and bear no name. I begin to think I might have to knock on doors and ask where the James family lives, but near the middle of the main drive I spot a dented mailbox, its flag bent, *The James's* scrawled in black paint on its rusty sides.

Its designated trailer is small, beige, and rusty too, with green trim. Its base is resting on blocks, the wheels useless. It reminds me of a pet bird with clipped wings. On the side of the trailer with the door, there are three windows. Red curtains patterned with tiny yellow flowers hang in the small window on one end; the curtains in the window at the other end are adorned with multicolored cartoon characters. The window between is tiny and frosted, as if for a bathroom. Below the raised door, cement blocks form steps. A flowerpot sitting to one side of them contains only a dried stick, all that remains of whatever plant it once held. Angry voices leak through the thin trailer walls as a man and a woman argue. There are other sounds too, strange ones I can't identify.

My heart beats wildly. I must summon all my courage to follow through with this. My plan may not work, but I must try—this could be the most important moment of my life. Taking a deep breath, I reach out and knock on the door.

The voices fall silent, although the other noise continues. A minute passes. I put out my hand to knock again, but the door opens, its hinges squealing.

A striking young woman stands in the doorway, looking out at me. Her auburn hair is swept up in a careless twist and stabbed with a hair stick, and there are faint smudges of mascara under the heavy lashes of her green eyes, which dart around as though she is expecting someone else. Can this be Melissa? Was I—*am I* this woman? I search for something familiar about her, but there is nothing.

"Yeah?" she says, holding up a hand to shield her eyes from the sun.

"I—my name is Sera. I'm looking for the Johnson family."

"You got the wrong place. Ain't no Johnsons here."

I unfold a small slip of paper as though to check something written on it. "Oh—I'm sorry, I must have written down the wrong address, then. I was supposed to talk to them about babysitting their two children. Just a temporary thing, hardly any pay—"

"Yeah, well, good luck."

She is about to close the door; I open my mouth to stop her as a small, pale slip of a girl appears at her side. "Who is it?" the girl asks quietly.

"Ain't nobody. Go on in and play. And turn that thing down; it's getting on my last nerve." The little girl remains at the woman's side, but sticks her thumb in her mouth.

"Is she yours?" I ask quickly.

The woman stares at me. I smile. "I'm only asking because she resembles you a little—I thought you might be sisters."

The woman's head jerks back and then she laughs—a harsh, edgy sound. "Sisters! Naw, the little brat's mine, all right. You sure you ain't trying to sell something?"

It's now or never. "I'm new in the area. I'm looking for a job—a regular babysitting job, that is."

The woman folds her arms across her chest. "We look like we got money for a babysitter?"

"No—I mean, the money isn't really important to me. Whatever you can afford; it doesn't matter."

The woman squints. "You on drugs or something?"

"My husband travels, you see, and I just want something worthwhile to do with my time during the day, that's all. I like being around children."

The little girl looks from me to her mother, thumb still in her mouth. The woman glances down at her and then gives her a swat on the behind. "I told you to stop that, didn't I." The girl's thumb comes out with a pop.

The woman looks at me again. "Well, my husband stays home all day—he's a cripple—so he watches the kids."

"I could always watch them for a little while to give him a break."

She shakes her head, unmoved. I'm beginning to panic, but I keep my voice calm. "I can also do some cooking and light cleaning."

This seems to perk her up a little, although she still seems skeptical. "Cleaning, huh?"

From inside the trailer comes a male voice. "Who is it?"

The woman shakes her head and turns it slightly to answer, "It's our new babysitter, that's who." She turns back to me. "So when can you start?"

"As soon as possible," I say, smiling with relief.

"How 'bout right now?"

"I'd like that."

She laughs and again shakes her head, and motions me to come inside, steering the little girl aside. "You sure you ain't on drugs?"

"None at all," I say.

"Well, honey, you *should* be."

I climb the cement block stairs and step into a small living room. Green shag carpet covers the floor; the walls are paneled; a worn gold sofa sits along the far wall opposite the door, a mismatched plaid chair beside it. I am standing near a large box on which two-dimensional cartoon images flicker endlessly while emitting loud, frantic sounds.

"For God's sake, turn that TV down, Hailey," the woman says to the girl, who runs to the box and turns a knob, causing the sounds to come out tinny and low. I have seen photographs of a television before, but not the real thing.

A small boy lies stomach-down on the sofa, his tear-streaked face turned toward me. He is pouting fiercely and scrunches up his face as though threatening to begin crying again at any moment. A man sits in a wheelchair next to the sofa, one hand resting on his lap, the other on the boy's head. He is young but unkempt, his hair and beard disheveled, his clothes worn and torn at one knee. His eyebrows are raised in surprise.

The woman turns to me, sighing. "I'm Melissa James—just call me Lissa. This here's my husband Gabe, that's Hailey, and that one over there hitchin', with a stomachache, is Bug."

"Bug?" I ask.

"Well, that ain't so much his name as his pastime. His real name's Billy. But trust me—you spend some time around him, you'll be calling him Bug, too."

Gabe clears his throat, looking at me. "And you are?"

"I'm Sera. I'm new to the area and—"

"And she's damn crazy enough, she's gonna help out around here for practically nothing for a while."

Gabe stares at me. "Is that right?"

"That's right," I say.

"Why?"

Melissa rolls her eyes. "Now, don't go asking her dumb questions like that. She might come to her senses and change her mind." She glances at the clock behind her in the tiny kitchen. "I have to rush off now—I know it's short notice, Gabe; I forgot to tell you—I told Albert I'd come in for a couple hours this afternoon."

Gabe and I both say, "You're *leaving*?"

"Shelley's been out sick and one of her Saturday regulars is going to some big bash somewhere tonight and wants the works—dye, cut, perm, style—and everybody else is off. It'll be a little extra money. She may be an old bag, but she's a *rich* old bag." Lissa turns to me. "We can work out the details later. You can get the kids some lunch and wash the dishes. Gabe can show you where everything is, right, Gabe?" Without waiting for an answer, she grabs her bag off the bar separating the kitchen and living room, then bends down and glances at her reflection in the toaster, swiping at her hair. "I look like shit, but there ain't no use in getting fixed up for an old bat, anyway." She takes out a cigarette and lights it with a match, which she extinguishes with a flick of her wrist and tosses into an ashtray already spilling over with butts.

Gabe rolls his chair to the door as she opens it. "When you get back, maybe we can go to a movie later, just you and me. *The Sting* is playing over at the Cinema..."

She stops, hand on the doorknob. "I don't know; I'm gonna be wore out and stink like horse piss after I give that old Miz Stutts a perm." She suddenly looks thoughtful. "On the other hand, it might be a good thing, us getting out of the house tonight—yeah, we'll make it a date. That is, if Sera can be here and watch the brats."

Gabe looks over at me. I inhale and smile. "That'd be good," I say. "I don't have a thing going on."

She sweeps out the door, slamming it behind her with a puff of smoke. Gabe and I are on either side of the door, Hailey still stands beside the TV, and Bug has sat up on the sofa to stare intently at me. This isn't exactly how I had imagined the first encounter with my past entity.

Gabe attempts a smile. "Lissa works at a beauty parlor across town."

Bug lets out a low, wet burp from the sofa. "Mama fitses hayew," he says, patting the top of his head.

Hailey says nothing, but slides her thumb back into her mouth.

"That's real nice," I say. Now that my plan succeeded and I am here, I don't know what to do. "Shall we have lunch?"

I move into the kitchen, searching it for a recognizable appliance, but I am totally mystified, and stand rubbing my hands together. Hailey rummages in the refrigerator and Bug climbs onto a chair with a bag of bread, trying to untwist the tie. I sag in relief as Hailey sets a store-bought container labeled *Tuna Fish Salad Sandwich Spread* and a knife on the table, and Gabe produces a bag with some kind of chips in it and tosses it alongside. I can tell they are used to the ritual that is their lunch.

Hailey gently grabs the bag of bread from Bug and untwists the tie herself. "I like tuna fish sandwiches," she says quietly.

Bug frowns and pounds on the table with two small, pudgy fists. "I can't git da bwead out, Daddy," he says. "Haywee won't *wet* me."

Gabe rolls his chair to the table. "Just sit down and wait for your food, Bug."

I begin spreading the tuna fish on slices of bread while Hailey digs out chips and puts them on paper plates. Soon we have a stack of sandwiches.

"Dig in," says Gabe. He gets a pitcher out of the refrigerator and pours four glasses of ice tea.

Since Hailey and Bug stare silently at me while they chew, I try not to wolf down my sandwich, but it's hard not to. I am ravenous. After all, I haven't eaten in over two hundred years. The tuna salad is unusual but tasty, the chips crunchy and salty, the tea cold and refreshing. Much better than the kelp dog I would be having for lunch at Cosmos.

When we're through I stack the paper plates and throw them away, put the chips and bread and carton of tuna away, and wash the glasses with hot water and the green liquid from the bottle Hailey hands me. I am aware of Gabe watching me from across the room, his arms folded.

"Now what?" I say as I hang up the towel.

Bug jumps up and down, making the trailer vibrate despite his small size. "We go to the beach an wook for shayows."

Hailey smiles shyly. "He likes to look for shells," she translates for me. "Can we?"

"That means walking on the beach. By the water," I say.

Gabe laughs. "That's where you find them, all right. I can only go so far in my chair, just to the end of the boardwalk out there. They both know how far they are allowed to go, if that's what's worrying you."

I look at Hailey and Bug, both staring up at me with eyes wide. Bug jumps up and down again. "I git my shayow bukkit," he says. He runs down the short hall and reappears with a small green pail, his face alight with excitement.

"Is it okay if I take my book with us?" Hailey asks Gabe.

"How about it, Sera?" he asks me.

"Sure, why not?" I say, my palms sweating. Just thinking about being near the largest body of water—*an ocean*—makes my heart race. But I don't know how to say no.

Hailey runs to get her book and we walk to the back door, which is on the wall opposite the kitchen. A wooden ramp with raised slats has been built to accommodate Gabe's chair, and he maneuvers down first, the rest of us following. We walk on a sandy path that winds between the trailers and downhill to the beach. I can hear the rush of the surf, the pounding breakers, and gulls crying out overhead. The breeze is cool and salty on my face and the air smells fresh.

When I first spot the water, I stop. The others hurry ahead of me, unaware that I am frozen to the spot and hyperventilating. All that dark blueness—surrounds me—traps me—drowns me. My heart thumps hard in my chest, and I feel as though I'm going to die.

"Whoa," Gabe shouts to the kids, then makes his way back to me. "You okay?" He's out of breath with the effort. "What's wrong? Sera?"

I plunk down in the sand where I am and put my head down between my bent knees. "I'm okay. I'm okay," is all I can manage.

The children have come back too. They stand looking at me and then at Gabe. "What's wrong?" Hailey asks.

"Wong?" echoes Bug.

"Are you sick, Sera?"

For a moment I was sure I would faint, but it's passed; I'm feeling better. Nevertheless, I admit, "I can't go out there."

"Why not?" Gabe's eyes hold concern.

"I just can't. I know it sounds silly, but I'm afraid of the water."

Bug drops his pail and plunks down on his hands and knees beside me, looking up at me closely. "Afwaid uh da wadew?"

I nod and wipe the sweat from my forehead. "I'm sorry, guys. I thought I could do it, but I don't think I can, after all. I have a phobia—a fear. Of the water."

Gabe whistles softly through his teeth. "Wow."

I nod, embarrassed. "I know."

Gabe looks out over the boardwalk and the beach beyond. "Do you think you can sit with me at the end of the boardwalk where I usually stop, and watch from there?" A few yards away from us, the boardwalk dead ends into a wider platform, like a deck, and a wooden bench sits along one side. Beyond is a wide expanse of beach and the Atlantic Ocean. "Better than that, you don't even have to look at the water—you can sit and face me."

I sit there for a minute, becoming used to the sounds around me. My pulse has slowed some; my anxiety has leveled out. "I can try," I say faintly.

"We'll try it, and then if it's too much you just say, and we'll head right back, no problem."

"Fair enough."

I get up on shaky legs and brush the sand off my jeans. We start down the path again with Gabe in the lead, Hailey and Bug each holding one of my hands, my eyes glued to the ground. Soon I'm sitting on the bench, the water crashing behind me, Gabe facing the beach where he can keep an eye on Hailey and Bug, who romp in the sand.

"You okay?" he says, his eyes kind.

"No, but I think I'm going to sit here for awhile anyway." I smile at him.

Gabe nods. "You wanna talk about it?"

"No."

"Fair enough." Gabe looks beyond me, watching his children play.

We sit for awhile, the breeze playing through our hair, me watching the gulls maneuvering gracefully on the wind. Then I catch him regarding me, smiling.

"You aren't from around here," he says simply.

Quickly I try to remember the story I have told Lissa. "My husband travels with his job—he's in sales—so we move around quite a bit. We're—"

"I know—new to the area. You don't have any children of your own, I take it."

"No," I say. I don't bother to tell him that it's impossible, that I will never have children, that hundreds of years of chemical pollution have rendered the human male almost sterile, the human female unable to carry a child to term without imminent danger to herself and her baby—and that most every child is now genetically created and developed completely outside the womb. It is very expensive, and even the wealthy are reluctant to try, as there are still many risks to the developing fetus. The number of the very young in our population is dwindling.

I was a grown woman before I learned from a longtime friend of my father's that my own mother resisted this laboratory method, which she thought cold and dispassionate, and opted for natural pregnancy despite strong opposition from her doctor and from my father, who feared for her. But she was always able to sway him, and over time he relented.

She took meticulous care of herself, careful to follow all special instructions her doctor gave her. And in spite of the danger, all seemed to go very well, right up until the time she suddenly went into labor at only six months. The doctors did everything they knew to save us both. But when the exhausted doctor finally stood before Father, all he could offer him was the life of his newborn child, which my mother had already named Sera. Me.

Gabe is watching his children. I can hear their laughter over the roar of the sea. "I know they're a handful," he says thoughtfully, "but frankly, I don't know what I'd do without them. Lissa, she's too hard on them, but she means well. We were awful young when she got pregnant with Hailey. Still in school.

"My family moved here from Ohio when I was in my freshman year of high school. And when I first laid eyes on Melissa Hardy, I thought she was just about the most beautiful creature that ever graced the earth. She took my breath away. I didn't think a girl like Lissa would ever go out with me, so I didn't even bother to ask for a long time. In fact, I took her best friend Cindy out for a couple of months, and when that fizzled out Lissa seemed to change toward me—acted interested, I guess—so I took the big leap and asked her to a movie, and she accepted.

"She's beautiful, all right, but her looks weren't the only thing about her that attracted me. She was always outgoing and unafraid. I guess she had a wild streak, but I liked that about her. One time, she pulled me under the bleachers and wanted to make love right there. I was scared someone would find us, but she—well, it was hard to say no." He laughs, embarrassed.

"Then one day she told me she was pregnant. I was scared about that, too—I even thought about running away, but only for a minute. Then I figured if I was any kind of a man, I was going to have to face up to my responsibilities, and we both managed to get through the rest of the school year. Lissa was never really into the pregnancy. I don't think she ever got finished sowing her wild oats—one minute she was a schoolgirl, the next a mother. It . . . was hard on her." He runs a hand over his rough beard.

"Then I was in a stupid accident, lost my legs, and it was like she had two of us to take care of. Bug—he was a surprise, all right. We took precautions and all, but it happens. You know, if it wasn't for him, I think she would have already left." He says this last sentence quietly, as though speaking to himself.

I blink, surprised. "Surely not, Gabe."

He looks at me. "Oh, it's true, all right. I may be a cripple, but I still have a mind. Maybe being confined to this chair makes me able to see things more clearly than I normally would. It's pretty obvious she hasn't been happy with me for a long time—maybe she never was; I don't know. I'm surprised she's stayed as long as she has. In some ways, she's already gone."

If Gabe is bitter, it doesn't show in his eyes. I see only sadness there.

"I'm so sorry."

He sits up. "I don't know why I'm boring you with this—I'm the one, should be sorry. We don't even know each other, and here I am spilling my guts to you. I can't believe I did that—I feel like an idiot."

"Probably no more than I do, for just about going hysterical at seeing the ocean."

Suddenly there is a burst of laughter as Bug and Hailey jump up on the platform. Bug turns his bucket bottoms up, spilling small shells onto the rough wood. "I got me sheyows, Daddy. Wook, Sewa."

I bend to examine them. They are shiny and wet, treasures from the sea. "How absolutely *beautiful*, Bug," I say. "They are the prettiest shells I ever saw."

He laughs his baby laugh and smiles big, his eyes shining. "I fine em aw mysayowf."

"Good job, buddy," Gabe says, laughing too.

Hailey has been waiting patiently and now steps forward, laying something at our feet. "See what I found?" she says, looking up at us.

"Wow," Gabe says.

When I look down, there is a little star lying on the deck, about the size of Hailey's small hand. Its spiny skin is almost yellow, its five gracefully tapered arms ending in blunt points. "Is it alive, Daddy?" Hailey asks him.

Gabe picks up the star and examines it closely. "No, hon, I don't think so."

Hailey opens her book, flips to a page, and slowly reads aloud, her finger tracing the words. "Starfish—phylum Echino-der-mata. Class Aster-oid-e-a."

"Where on earth did you learn to read like that, Hailey?" I say, stunned.

"My Daddy taught me," she says, grinning proudly, taking the starfish from her father. "The book says that some species of starfish have as many as forty arms, and they live in all the world's oceans."

Gabe whistles. "Can you imagine that?"

Hailey continues, "They don't even have a brain—"

"Tarfeesh got no bwain," Bug interrupts.

"—But if they lose one of their arms, they can grow a *new* one. And if a starfish is cut in two, it'll grow into two starfish."

"They can grow an arm *right back*, you say?" Gabe says. For a moment he is thoughtful, then his eyes sparkle with mischief. He pokes Hailey gently on the nose. "I guess that's why you never saw a starfish in a wheelchair," he says.

Everyone looks at him for a moment, then he bursts into gales of hearty laughter, and we all join him.

Seeing Hailey like this, her eyes alight and her face animated—she seems a different little girl than the timid, pale one I first saw standing next to her mother at the door. I haven't been around many young children, but she seems startlingly bright for a seven-year-old child—so eager to learn. She is patient and good with her little brother. I realize that I haven't seen her sucking her thumb all afternoon. I think of Lissa and wonder if she really knows her own daughter at all.

"Wanna git more sheyows," Bug says, and grabs his empty pail.

"Maybe we oughta go on back now," Gabe says, looking at me with raised eyebrows.

"I'm okay if you want to stay a little longer. Just keep talking—it keeps my mind off you know what," I say.

"Then knock yourselves out. Just stay where you're supposed to," he tells the kids.

Hailey sets her book down on the bench and they go running onto the beach, Bug yelling, "Tarfeesh got no bwains, tarfeesh got no bwains," at the top of his voice, his chubby legs pumping wildly through the sand and his little green pail bumping against him as he runs. Hailey twirls round and round, hair flying, as though she soars with the gulls.

I can feel the ocean at my back and the spray in the wind. "Talk to me, please, Gabe."

"I love watching the kids run," Gabe says. He lifts one of his legs from the footrest of the chair with both arms, and slowly sets it down again. He repeats this with the other leg. "Gotta keep the circulation going," he says. "My legs have been useless for about seven years now. You'd think I'd have gotten used to being a cripple, but I still can't really believe it. Other people dream they can fly, I dream I can walk. Sometimes I even dream I'm running. I can feel my legs moving fast under me, my feet hitting the ground, and I wake up panting hard, like I've been running a marathon. And it makes me think, just for a minute, that if I can do it in my dreams, why not for real? But I know better, that even though my brain still knows how, there's a short circuit to my legs. So it's never gonna happen."

It's easy to see I have taken the technology in my time for granted; I have never seen anyone unable to walk, and I can't imagine how it must feel. "How did it happen, Gabe?"

"You sure you want to hear about it?"

I nod. "If it doesn't bother you too much to talk about it."

"I don't know; I never do." He laughs a pained laugh. "Here goes . . .

"In my senior year of high school, a few of us guys were going out after a basketball game; we had just beat our biggest rival fifty-five to thirty-nine—man, it was a great game. We were still pumped and excited when we drove up the highway to get a burger somewhere. I remember it was raining and we were still running our mouths about the game and everything, and then—" Gabe shrugs and throws up his hands "—nothing. I can't remember anything after that. I don't even remember much about those first days in the hospital. I had a concussion and was cut up pretty bad, and paralyzed from a back injury. The other guys, they didn't make it—just my best bud old Neil and me. Neil managed to pull through for a while, but he never came out of the coma, and then after a few months he just died. I didn't make it to any of the funerals."

Gabe stops, his eyes watering. He blinks and then smiles. "So there's not really much to tell, is there? Except I wondered for a long time why I had to be the one that made it. It didn't seem right, you know? Then after the kids were born, I figured I was supposed to be here for them. Even if I wasn't worth much else, I was a father, and that meant something. *Means* something."

"You're a great dad, Gabe." I smile at him. "Anyone can see that."

His face lights up and he grins. "Thanks."

He takes a small piece of wood and a pocketknife out of his shirt pocket. He opens the knife and begins to carve with it. Wood shavings fall at his feet. "This is fairly soft wood," he says. "The kids like me to whittle little toys for them sometimes, so I keep some handy."

He works with the knife, turning the piece of wood this way and that. "I used to like Shop in school—working with wood, you know. I like the feel of it in my hands. I guess this is something I can do sitting down, and it doesn't cost much. That's definitely a plus."

I watch for a long while, fascinated, as the edge of his sharp knife bites into the soft wood, taking carefully measured chunks of the block away here and there, then taking away the rough edges and leaving a smooth, rounded shape instead. Sometimes he works with the edge of the blade and sometimes he uses the point, chiseling little impressions into the surface, flicking the small shavings away with his fingers, blowing the dust away. There is a pleasant focus about Gabe as he whittles, his features moving a little as he works. Occasionally he glances up to check his kids.

"You haven't told me much about yourself," he finally says, still carving.

"There isn't much to tell that would be very interesting."

"I find that hard to believe," he says, smiling. "You have an air about you—something I can't quite put my finger on, something unusual. Different. Exotic. I don't really know what I mean, but there's something there."

"I forget you can see more clearly than most," I say, and he laughs.

"Okay, then," I say, giving up. "I was born in a very large city—Chicago. My mother died when I was born, my father raised me, I flunked out of medical school, I got married to a man in sales—Thomas—we have no children, no pets, he travels a lot, I'm bored, and that's about it. Nothing exotic."

Gabe blows on the carving again. "What line of sales is your husband Thomas in?"

I look around frantically, my eyes coming to rest on his pocketknife. "He's in cutlery."

Gabe looks up. "Cutlery."

"That's right. It's a very hot item right now."

"I'm sure it is," he says, his eyes twinkling.

"I bet the children are getting thirsty," I say, rising from the bench. "Can we go back now?"

"Sure thing—I'm about finished with this." Gabe holds out the small carving he has done. "Take it," he says. "It's yours."

I take it and hold it up, unable to stifle a gasp. It's a tiny starfish, complete with five graceful arms and spiny skin. "It's fantastic, Gabe." I turn it over and over in my hands, totally enthralled. "It could be the real thing."

"Naw," he says, gushing a little. He folds his knife and puts it back in his pocket.

"*Yes*. It's so intricately detailed and real. I've never seen anything so grand. You have true talent."

"You really think so?" He looks surprised.

"I really do."

We look at each other for a moment, and then he looks away and clears his throat. "Well, I'd better get back and get ready for my date tonight. It's gonna take a while."

"Right," I say.

"Let's go, kids," he yells to them. They come running, giggling and breathless, and the four of us make our way back up the sand path to the trailer. The sun hangs low in the late afternoon sky.

* * *

"If you need to go home and get anything or do anything, you can go on while I'm getting ready," Gabe tells me. Hailey is coloring in a coloring book, and Bug lies sleeping on the floor in front of the television, worn out after his romp on the beach.

"They'll be fine," he adds. I don't want to monopolize all your time."

"There are a few things I need to do," I say. "I'll be back in a couple hours."

I leave the trailer and walk back through the trailer park and onto Oak again, heading into town. The smell of meat cooking on a charcoal grill in someone's backyard wafts through the air, and my mouth waters. My clothes feel dirty, and sticky from the salty air. I only have a few hours, so I stop downtown at a dress shop and buy a blue dress with short sleeves and a hem that's fashionably above my knees, along with some under things. I walk farther down to a Shell gas station and go into the ladies' restroom to wash up and change into my new clothes, stuffing the dirty ones into the trash.

I call Dr. Moore and Dr. Weiss on my communicator band. They are glad to hear from me. "We've been monitoring the movements of your energy signature every step of the way, Sera," Dr. Moore tells me, the audio signal full of static. "You must have located your past entity by now."

"Yes." I tell them what has happened so far, from the first encounter with Willie to the last words with Gabe, omitting the part about telling Willie who I really am.

"Excellent observations," says Dr. Weiss.

"You understand the drowning took place—takes place—tomorrow morning at precisely 10:15 a.m.," Dr. Moore says calmly.

"I understand. Right now I'm just trying to stay close by. Melissa is hard to monitor, but I'll manage."

"Be careful, Sera," Dr. Moore says. "We're here if you need us. Let us know the moment something happens, so we can bring you back safely."

"Right," I say. I know the project would be in hot water if something were to go wrong. "Don't worry."

I leave the gas station, cross the street, and go down to the Grille, where I order three large cheeseburgers and two large chocolate shakes. I have never eaten these things before, but they look and smell divine as I study the plates sitting in front of the diners seated in the booths. I pay for them, then walk back down Oak Street and then over to Third Street.

After first looking around to see if anyone is watching, I duck into the small alley beside the pawnshop, which is now closed. I approach the old box, hearing nothing but the traffic on the street behind me, and an ancient airplane grinding high overhead.

"Willie? Anybody home?" I whisper. No answer. Then the curtain flutters and a small white muzzle appears, followed by a black mask and floppy ears.

"Who's there?" a deep, raspy voice calls from within.

"It's me, Willie. Sera. Remember me?"

Now he appears in the little cutout door, too. "Of course I remember you, child. I was getting nervous that it might be them aliens. You can't be too careful." He looks at the bag in my hand. "What you got there?"

"You gave me shelter," I say, "so I owe you dinner. All right?"

He looks at me for a moment, confused. Then he laughs. "All right, then. Come inside and I'll set up the dinner table for two."

"Three," I say, gently tickling Goblin's ears. He looks at the bag and licks his chops. I crawl into the box and we all tuck ourselves into our respective corners, stretching our legs out the best we can. The little shells click against one another overhead.

I dig the burgers out of the bag, hand Willie his along with a milkshake and a plastic spoon, and then let Willie give Goblin his own burger, which he snarfs down without hesitation.

Willie laughs. "He ain't got the manners God give a flea. Goblin, don't you know it ain't polite to eat so fast?" Then he takes a big bite out of his own burger; catsup drips onto his scraggly beard.

"I don't know what this is," I say, pointing to my own burger, "but it's the best thing I've ever tasted in my life."

Willie stares at me. "Ain't you folks got cheeseburgers where you're from?"

I shake my head. "Most things are made from seaweed and kelp. It's a rare thing to find meat, and when you do, it's nothing like this. It's usually stringy and chewy."

It's Willie's turn to shake his head. "Now, that's the saddest thing I heard in a long time, when folks ain't got a decent burger to eat."

We are silent in the box; the only sounds are the chewing and swallowing of the truly hungry. Willie finishes his last bite, wipes his mouth on his sleeve, and then works on his chocolate milkshake, spooning the melted cold stuff into his mouth so fast, he has to stop for a minute and hold his aching head. I have to admit I'm no better, almost keeping up with them both.

"There's something about your time that makes me very hungry," I say.

"I know just what you mean," Willie says. "We're much obliged, Miss Sera, me and Goblin. You know, it's been quite a day. First I find myself a ten-dollar bill and buy us a slice of sweet potato pie, then a very nice visitor from the future drops in and keeps us company on a rainy day, and now we got us a fine dinner. It's been a day filled with the Lord's sweet blessings, truly now."

Willie leans back and pats his stomach. "I'm gonna have to walk some of this off later on. Goblin and me haven't been out all day, have we, boy? He wasn't feeling too well this morning, you see. But I believe he's starting to perk right up."

To me, the little dog looks fine. It's Willie who looks tired and drawn, though he seems in good spirits.

"Tell me about your day, now," he says. "Did you find that young lady you were looking for?"

I tell Willie about meeting Lissa at the trailer park, and about Gabe and Hailey and Bug, and our trip to the beach.

"You've taken a shining to them, have you?" he asks.

I sigh and lean back too, my stomach uncomfortably full. "I still don't really know them, of course. Gabe . . . he seems kind of tragic in one way, yet in other ways I think he's so—*real*. So wise. But Hailey and Bug—you should have seen them out there at the beach. They're so full of life and fun, I can't help but smile when I think of them. And Lissa, I don't know. *She's* supposed to be *me*—we're supposed to be *one and the same person*, only in different bodies and in different times. I thought I would be drawn to her because of that. Yet I don't recognize anything about her at all that seems like me. Don't get me wrong—I know I'm not perfect or anything. But to tell you the truth, I don't think I even *like* her very much. Is that possible?"

Willie looks thoughtful, letting out a little burp. "I don't know, Sera. I can tell you there's been many times I haven't liked myself much. Not at all. Fact is, there's been times I wasn't sure who Willie really was. You'd be better off to ask somebody else a question like that, now."

I reach up and gently push one of the shells with my finger. It swings back and forth on its string, spilling its good luck. "You know, I'd give just about anything to have what Lissa has. And she isn't happy at all, according to Gabe."

Willie sighs. "Well, that there's what you call irony—when you want something so bad it hurts, but it just ain't meant to be."

I look up at his tired face, at his meager surroundings. "This must all seem so frivolous to you, Willie," I say quietly.

"Ain't nothing frivolous when it come to the heart, child. When I was a boy and something wouldn't go the way I wanted and I'd get all mad and upset with people, my papa would set me down and tell me, 'Folks just all trying to live, son, each in their own way.' Maybe you understand why somebody is the way they is, and maybe you don't understand them at all. But folks all got their own ways about them—good and bad. And that's all there is to it in this life, you know. We all just trying to find our way."

I think about what he has said, and I think about Father—if only he had found it in himself to tell me things like that. I think about what it will be like for Willie during the stifling heat of the coming summer, and the numbing cold of the winter to follow. I wonder if there can be many more of either for him.

If he'll take it, I decide to leave him what money I have left over before I have to go home. That means I will see him again before I leave, in order to give it to him. I long to take Willie back with me, but it's impossible for Krate to retrieve a past entity because the energy signature is different somehow—that's what they said.

"I wish . . ." I begin.

"What's that?"

"Never mind."

Willie smiles, and it's almost as if he's read my thoughts. "Now, don't you go worrying about old Willie none. I been out here a long time, now. I know how to take care of myself."

We're quiet for a while, and then I check my Mickey Mouse watch. His hands say 6:30 p.m. "I have to go now," I say. "I have to go back to the trailer and try to keep track of Lissa until—well, until tomorrow morning. I don't know when I'll be back, but I promise I'll try to see you again sometime before I have to go home."

Willie leans forward, his eyebrows raised in concern. "Are you sure you'll be able to handle what's gonna happen tomorrow? If your Dr. Moore is right, it's already in the cards that woman gonna drown—ain't nothing gonna change that. *You gonna watch somebody die, Sera.* And that family gonna be without that young woman and suffer because of it, no matter what their lives seem like to you. I'm only a old bum, but seems to me that ain't no way to keep a bad dream away."

The reality of Lissa's impending death is beginning to hit me now, and my old self-doubts return. "I don't know what's going to happen tomorrow, Willie. I know if I think about it too hard, I'll want to help her, and that's forbidden. I just feel compelled to be there when it happens, right or wrong—that's all I know. Then I'll go home, taking with me whatever I have to from it, good or bad. And if nothing else, I'll have met *you*. That was definitely worth the trip."

Willie's eyes seem to water a bit, and Goblin sits up suddenly beside him, burping softly. "Then you just remember old Willie told you to take good care of yourself," he says. "And Goblin and me, we'll be here whenever it is you come back."

When I leave the Palace and head down the street, I walk down a couple of blocks and then turn around to see Willie heading down the street the other way, trudging slowly and stiffly like an old man but with his head up, little Goblin limping closely at his side.

6:45 p.m.

Hailey answers the door with a wide grin, her mouth and tongue purple. "Hi Sera," she says softly.

"Well, hi yourself," I say, grinning too. "What in the world is that on your face?"

"Daddy fed us some supper and he let me have some grape juice after," she replies. "Bug doesn't like it, but I do."

I step into the trailer, where Bug stands in front of the television, a cookie in one pudgy hand, his mouth wet with soggy crumbs and his plump cheeks flushed. His face lights up when he sees me, and he comes running. "Sewa, Sewa, Sewa," he yells, hugging my legs.

I kneel down and hug them both. "Wow—I have never had such a welcome, ever before."

"Now, I find that hard to believe." Gabe's voice comes from the kitchen. When he enters the living room, the three of us stare at him. He has been transformed. He is now clean-shaven, his scraggly growth of beard gone. His hair is clean and neatly combed, and he wears a blue shirt with a nice pair of tan slacks.

"Wow," is all I can think of to say.

Hailey giggles. "Is that really you, Daddy?"

Bug stares, his eyes wide. "*Yooo*, Daddy?"

Gabe laughs, his face red. "I just thought, if I'm going on a real date tonight, I should dress like it."

I whistle. "Well, any girl would be proud to go out with a handsome guy like you. Right, Hailey?"

"Right," she says, her eyes sparkling with pride for her father.

He responds with an embarrassed smile. "I fed the kids and they can play for awhile before bedtime."

"Did Lissa call?" I ask. I'm surprised she isn't home yet. Perhaps it takes longer to do a perm than I thought.

"No, but it's more like her to just show up," Gabe says. "If she gets home in the next hour, she'll still have time to get cleaned up for the movie. She must have grabbed a bite to eat at the little joint next door to the beauty parlor. She does that sometimes."

I nod and look at the kids. "Let's see what kind of fun we can have before bedtime, then, shall we?"

"Yeah," they yell in unison.

First we play a game of catch in the small yard with a big, orange-speckled ball that is almost as big as Bug; he has to spread his short arms as wide as he can just to pick it up and hold onto it. Then he gives it a great heave, opening his arms, and the ball drops only a foot in front of him.

His face screws into a pout. "I can't thwow da baw, Sewa."

"You're doing just fine, Bug. Why don't you try rolling it instead?"

He drops the ball onto the ground and pushes it with both hands, but it still doesn't go very far. He collapses onto the ground and begins to cry.

"Just *kick* it, Bug—like this," Hailey says, showing him.

Bug pouts and stares at the ball for a moment, then stands. I hold my breath as he runs toward it for all he's worth, his wide eyes focused and determined. He swings a short leg out, catching the ball square, and it arcs into the air and bounces once before coming to a stop in the grass.

"You did it, you did it," Hailey and I yell together, and Bug grins, then self-consciously pulls his shirt up over his face.

So now we play kick the ball, Hailey and I trying not to kick it too far, until we collapse onto the ground, laughing and out of breath. I look up to see Gabe watching, smiling, from the open door. "They're quite the little kickers," I say. "And they're wearing me out already."

Gabe laughs. "Tell me about it." He looks down the road, his features becoming tense. I glance at my watch and see that it's already after seven, and the movie starts in half an hour.

I turn to Hailey and Bug, sprawled on the grass beside me. "Why don't we go inside now and you can get your baths, and then I'll tell you a bedtime story. How does that sound?"

"You can weed da one wif da dwaggin in it, Sewa?" Bug asks me.

I gently muss his fine, curly hair. "We'll see."

As I herd the kids to their tiny room, Gabe picks up the phone on the table beside the sofa and punches numbers. "I'm calling the beauty parlor and see what's up," he says.

Hailey finds their pajamas and Bug flops onto his narrow bed. "I don't *wanna* take no baf," he says.

"You have to, Bug," his sister tells him, dumping his pajamas on top of him.

"Don't forget I'm going to tell you a story when you get all tucked into bed," I say.

He looks up at me. "Weew it have a dwaggin in it, or a dog?"

Hailey giggles. "He just likes animal stories; it doesn't matter what kind of animal it is," she explains.

I turn to him. "Then it will definitely have an animal in it. You'll have to *guess* what it is."

Bug gets up and runs into the bathroom. "I get a baf now, Sewa," he calls, and Hailey and I wink at each other.

Half an hour later, I gently close the door to the tiny room and walk into the living room where Gabe sits staring into space.

"No answer," he says simply.

"Where can she be, Gabe?" I feel a sudden pang of worry. What if something has gone wrong? What if EyeCom got the time of death wrong and it's already happened? And whenever it does, what will happen to Gabe, Hailey, and Bug? Who will watch over them?

I sit down slowly on one end of the worn sofa. In such an incredibly short time, I have begun to feel that this small family is part of me—everyone but Lissa, that is. *Irony was the word Willie used.* Now how will I ever leave them?

Gabe is looking at me, an odd expression on his face. "Are you all right, Sera?"

"Yes, of course."

He shakes his head. "It's after eight. The movie started already."

"I hope nothing has happened . . ."

"She *forgot*—that's what happened."

"I'm sorry, Gabe."

He hits the arm of his chair and exhales slowly and deliberately. "Forget about the movie. I just get so *angry* sometimes. With Lissa. She doesn't even *try*." He looks down at his nice clothes. "Who am I kidding? I might as well go change back into my old duds—I'm just wrinkling these for nothing." He swipes a hand over his face in a habitual gesture, and realizes anew that he is clean-shaven. He laughs bitterly. "At least it'll all grow back, huh?"

I don't know how to comfort him, so I'm silent as he makes his way to the back room to change.

5

Lissa

It's just like my mother always said: "First things first." Here I got *important* things going on, but no—I have to cater to old lady Stutts with her blue hair and red nose. 'Bout as soon as I get the door unlocked, she struts into the Beauty Barn like an old hen and squeezes her big fat ass into my chair and expects me to be her little hand servant—*Can you get me a glass of water, can you wipe off my eyes, can you turn down that dryer; it's too hot . . .*

She near about drives me crazy while I'm working on her dye job, and I can hardly wait till the moment I can finally rip those perm rods out of her hair and whip it up into a frigging nest like she likes. And I have to act like I don't mind doing it so she'll give me a decent tip after—five dollars, maybe.

Takes a while to get them perm rods in her hair. She likes her perm nice and tight, so I use the little ones. While I'm rolling, my mind tends to wander, and soon I'm thinking about Brian, but I try to push that out of my mind for now. It just makes me nervous. Then I'm thinking about that babysitter girl. Seems like there's a lot of weird things going on lately. I mean, how many times you gonna find somebody crazy enough to want to watch your kids, much less for *next to nothing*? Don't make sense to me. Seems like there's gotta be a catch. I know there's some people that like kids and all. I just never personally ran into one.

'Cept for Gabe, of course. He dotes on them kids so much sometimes, I think they don't even know they have a mother. Here I stand on my two feet and work my fingers to the bone to provide for all three of them, and they're always whining about something. First thing when I walk through that door, that's what they do. Sometimes I wonder how it is they remember to breathe if I'm not there. They're probably all turning blue right now.

I'm thinking about that babysitter, with her zombie-pale skin—almost as pale as Becka—and her dark eyes and her dark hair. She don't look like she's from around here. Maybe another country or something; I don't have a clue. She ain't movie star gorgeous, but she's different. I think maybe I could give her shiny dark hair a good cut, and maybe I wouldn't have to pay her for watching the kids at all. Kind of like a trade. I don't know what got into me, telling her I'd pay her for babysitting and cleaning, even if she don't want nothing much. I must have a screw loose.

I'm trying to save up a wad of cash I can use to leave this stinking place. I ain't told anybody, but last October I opened me a savings account in my name only, and I got a hundred and fifty dollars saved up. It's taken me a while to do it, but it makes me feel good to know it's there, money all my own. And someday when I have enough—well, someday . . .

Then I'm thinking, there's that babysitter setting there with my kids and my *husband*, too, and that makes me feel kind of funny. Why, I don't know. Maybe I just don't like competition there in my own house, not that she rates. Then I laugh out loud, 'cause I know, ain't no woman crazy enough to want a cripple like Gabe.

I practically forget old lady Stutts is setting right there when I laugh, and she looks up from the chair at my reflection and squints, but she don't say nothing.

So I'm moving right along; I put her under the dryer again for a while (*Can you hand me that magazine—no, not that one, that one . . .*) and I begin to see the light at the end of the tunnel. The sooner I get out of here, the better. Then I can find out what's going on from Cindy.

The only thing is, halfway through the comb-out, I notice something funny about my left hand. Then it dawns on me—my wedding ring is gone. I stand there staring at the white place where it should be until I remember taking it off last night and tucking it down into the pocket of my dress, right before I walked up to the bar.

Old lady Stutts looks at me in the mirror and says, "What's wrong?"

"Nothing."

I'm relieved for a minute until I think, what if my ring fell out with all that jostling and carrying on in the bus, me pulling the dress off over my head and all, and pitching it into the corner? But what really sets my teeth on edge is, what if it somehow fell into the parking lot, or worse—*what if it fell into Brian's truck when I was sitting in it?*

Old lady Stutts is still staring up at me in the mirror. "Something's *wrong* with you, young woman. Is it my hair? Didn't my perm turn out all right?"

I throw down the rat-tail comb I'm using to tease the queen's hair; it clatters on the counter as I run for the door.

The old bat screams, "Well, where are you *going to?*"

And I take the time to stop and say, "I forgot something. Don't get your panties all in a wad, just set right there and I'll be right back." 'Cause there ain't no use in getting her all mad and risk losing my tip if I don't have to. Then I run outside to the VW bus.

I fling open its squeaky doors and start searching every nook and cranny down on my hands and knees, so close I'm breathing the musty smell wafting up from the dirty carpet. When I spy something shiny under a seat I think I've found it for a moment, but turns out it's only an old silver gum wrapper. Finally I set down on the floor and realize that ring ain't in the bus. "It's gotta still be in the pocket of the dress I was wearing," I say out loud. Then I remember digging deep down in that pocket for a tissue to blow my nose with while I was driving home from the bar, but there wasn't nothing in there—no tissue, no nothing.

That's when I can feel my face getting all hot as I think about the police finding my ring at the murder scene. In my mind's eye, I can see a chalk outline of Brian's body, naked except for its boots, and a detective scooping up that ring—my ring—from the ground next to it and holding it up so he can see the inscription inside it: *To Lissa, Love Always, Gabe.* Then he shows it to the other policemen and they nod and wink and put it into an evidence bag to dust it for prints and keep it safe for my upcoming murder trial. My eyes get big and my forehead breaks out in a cold sweat. But maybe they haven't found it yet. Maybe it's lying out there in the gravel and nobody's seen it.

I gotta call Cindy. I run back into the beauty parlor and Miz Stutts is setting there glaring at me with her hair all teased up and out like a deranged clown, but I don't have time to mess with it. I whip her chair around so she can't see herself in the mirror and brush all that frizz into a blob of cotton at the top of her head and tie a ribbon around it. "There, you're all done," I say, out of breath, and grab her up out of that chair and lead her toward the door, still wearing the plastic bib over her dress.

"Well, what about your money?" she says, balking at the door.

"Forget it—it's a weekend special," I say. "You're the frigging Customer of the Month."

She winches them fat cheeks up into a smile and puts her hand up to feel her new coif, but I grab her hand and shake it instead and push her out the door. "Hurry up before I change my mind," I tell her, and she rushes off, barely stealing a backward glance.

"Cheap old bat," I say and lock the door, flip over the sign so it says *Closed*, and yank down the shade.

I run to the phone and punch in Cindy's number and wait and wait, but of course there ain't no answer. Then I remember something about a church dinner, so I call information and ask for the number and then I call out there to Third Baptist on Tidewater Street where her Auntie Ada goes. Some old mummified woman answers and I ask for Cindy, and she hems and haws around, asking who's calling, and I tell her it ain't any of her business, if she really wants to know. She gets kind of huffy but she finally goes to look for Cindy.

I'm standing there tapping my foot and listening for a siren in the distance, thinking I could use the back door to make my escape at the first sound. But all I can hear is the clatter of dishes and chatter coming from the phone.

Finally Cindy picks it up. "Hello?"

"What took you so damn long?" I yell at her.

"Lissa?"

"Stop saying my name, will you? Who else is gonna be calling you out there? I need to know, did you ever hear anything else about—you know what?"

"I ain't heard a thing, Lissa. I mean—uh, Sylvia."

"Are you sure? Haven't they done the autopsy or nothing?"

"I don't know. I've been here all day, helping get all this shit set up."

I sigh and lean back against the wall. "I lost my wedding ring last night, Cindy. Can you believe it? I don't know where it is. For all I know, it could be setting in the police station. But I'm hoping maybe it's in the parking lot at the bar."

"How the hell could you do that, Lissa? *Lord.*"

"I don't know, *I don't know.*"

"Well, you're gonna have to go look for it, that's all."

"I guess I ain't got any choice. But I can't risk anybody recognizing the bus. You gotta drive me out there to the Riverside Bar, Cindy. Now."

Cindy's voice gets all high when she's upset, which I hate. "I can't just pick up and leave Auntie Ada, Lissa. Who's gonna help clean up and carry her casserole dish and drive her home after? Try Becka, she'll do it."

"Becka doesn't know anything about this, and I don't think I want to tell her—she wouldn't understand. Besides, she's probably working a shift at the hospital."

Cindy sighs. "I'm sorry, Lissa, Auntie Ada is counting on me. She's old."

"Well, which is more important—Auntie Ada and a dumb old church dinner or your best friend in all the world frying in the electric chair?"

Cindy has to think about that for a minute.

"Cindy?" I say. "*Dammit.*"

"All right, all right. I'll tell Auntie Ada I got an errand to run and come pick you up, and drop you off at the bar. That's all I can do. I *mean* it."

"Hurry up, then. I'll be waiting here at the beauty shop. And bring me a plate of that church food—I'm starving."

Fifteen minutes later I'm peering out at the street from behind the shade, on pins and needles and about to lose my mind, when Cindy pulls up out front in her car. I slip out the door and get in beside her. "Just *go*," I yell at her, feeling like we've robbed a bank or something and this is the getaway car.

"All right, all right," she says, pulling the car away from the curb so fast, the tires screech. I look over at her and she's screwing up her nose and taking looks at me. "*Damn*, you stink."

"It's the perm," I tell her. "I can't help that right now. Just drive, will you?"

She hands me a rolled-up napkin, and I open it up and there's a chicken leg. "That's all you brought me, is a little, skinny ass chicken leg?"

Cindy laughs her hoarse laugh. "That's all that was left outa all that food. That and the brussels sprouts."

"*Damn*. What are they, a bunch of buzzards?"

Cindy's quiet for a minute while I'm chewing. Then she looks over at me, her eyes wide. "What are you gonna do if you can't find your ring, Lissa? What if the police already have it and they have a warrant out for you, and they're looking for you right now? What if they're over at the bar, waiting with handcuffs for you to come looking for it?"

I look at her. She's all spiffed up, not a hair out of place, fresh from a church social—and I'm sitting here all dirty and sweaty and stinking like horse piss. "Damn, Cindy, ain't you just Miss Sunshine this evening?" I say all cheerful-like, my cheeks puffed out with chicken so my words are muffled some. "Wait—you forgot to slip the noose around my neck."

She glances at me. "I'm sorry, I guess I was just thinking out loud, is all. I don't know what got into me. Forget it."

I stare at the road ahead. It's just starting to get dark, when the edges of things start getting all fuzzy-like. "Hell, that's all right," I tell her, wiping the grease off my mouth and fingers with the napkin. "You didn't bring up anything I haven't already thought of myself. The thing is, I gotta look for it, though. I gotta get my hands on that ring, if there's still a chance. I'm dead if it gets into the wrong hands."

Cindy's acting spooked, shifting around all nervous-like and shit. "Are you sure Brian was still alive last night when you left him?" she asks. "I mean, is there a chance that—well, that—"

"I didn't kill him, Cindy, if that's what you mean."

"But maybe it was an accident—"

"He was *alive*. I'm ninety-nine percent sure. He either just bought it from natural causes, or else somebody must have come and killed him after I left, is all I can figure."

"That just don't make no sense, Lissa. I mean, think about it—somebody just happening upon a drunk man passed out on the ground and then killing him, I mean."

"Yeah, that bothered me too," I say, cupping my chin in my thumb and index finger. "Unless . . ."

"Unless what, Lissa?"

"Unless they was getting his money out of his wallet, and . . . *Okay*—now picture this." I'm getting all excited. "He's still lying on the ground shit-faced, you see, only now he's starting to come to; he's still groggy, but awake enough that he can see whoever it is standing there digging his wallet out of his pants, which were lying next to him in a heap—and see him good enough that he'd be able to identify him to the cops. So the thief has no choice—he *has* to take Brian out. Yeah, that could be it."

Cindy purses her lips and nods. "But, who is it? Who's gonna be out there, that time of night?"

"How the hell should I know? Some drunk, probably, looking for someplace to piss, and he found himself a real opportunity instead. Brian's the kind of guy, he'd probably carry a few hundred in his wallet at a time. I bet he had a wad of money on him."

She shrugs. "I don't know, it still sounds kind of weird to me."

I slump down in the seat a little and wish I could lie down and go to sleep. "Well, weirder things have happened."

As we turn down the road leading to the bar, I close my eyes, dreaming out loud. "If I had myself a wad of money, I sure as hell wouldn't stick around here. I'd be gone far away from this dump of a town. I should have left a long time ago, and I wouldn't be in this mess."

"Yeah? And go where?"

"I don't know—somewhere with some life to it. Somewhere nobody expects nothing from me. Somewhere there ain't no messes to clean up all the time. That's where." I open my eyes and tell Cindy to slow down and stop at the crest of the hill just up the road from the bar. I crane my neck to see what I can see. "What do you think?"

"I think the murder must have been good for business—the place is *packed*."

"I don't see any cops. You?"

Cindy peers around, her eyes squinted. "Naw, but there's more parking around back, too, you know. We can't see it from here."

I chew on my thumbnail. "There's so many cars and trucks in that parking lot, I ain't gonna be able to find shit."

Cindy frowns. "Yeah, but you'll be able to hide in amongst them."

We sit still for a minute. Then Cindy sighs. "I gotta go, Lissa. I gotta go buy some cigarettes."

"How can you think about smoking at a time like this?" I ask, wishing I had one right now, myself.

She looks at me, still frowning. "'Cause I told Auntie Ada I had to go out and buy some cigarettes, that's why. If I go back to the church without any, she's gonna be suspicious."

I'm getting real sick of hearing about Cindy's Auntie Ada. "I don't see why you can't take a few more of your precious minutes and help me look, for God's sake. It would take half as long, with two of us out there." I hate how my voice is starting to sound all whiny, like Cindy's, but I can't help it.

Cindy sighs and rolls her eyes back into her bleached head. "It ain't always about *you*, Lissa. Everything ain't just about you, you, you. You can't *always* be thinking about yourself. You gotta think of others too, sometimes. Take my Great Auntie Ada. That woman is my only aunt, Lissa, and she turned ninety-two last month. *Ninety-two years old.* And when she passes on, she's gonna leave her favorite niece a shitload of money. Doesn't that mean anything to you at all?"

She puts both hands on the steering wheel and looks straight ahead. "Now, I done you a favor, driving you out here. I told you on the phone I could only drop you off, and that's what I'm gonna do."

I sit there in my misery and shake my head. If I didn't know better, it's almost like she wants me to get caught. "All right, all right," I say. "At least drop me off closer than this. I'm gonna look conspicuous enough as it is."

We drive down on past the bar, do a U-turn, and she stops the car on the street at the parking lot, not even bothering to turn in. I open the door and get out and slam it shut.

"Good luck," Cindy says through the open window. "I hope you find it."

I'm still furious at her so I just throw up my hands and she drives off, sending gravel flying every which way.

I kick at the gravel, too. "Well, be sure and give my love to Auntie Ada," I yell after her.

As I watch her taillights disappear over the hill, it occurs to me that I have no idea how I'm going to get home. Not only that, but I don't have a flashlight and it's getting dark. I'm going to play hell, finding anything in these conditions.

People are still arriving and grabbing the few remaining parking spaces, and music is booming out through the walls of the damn place like it's gonna explode. But I ain't seen the first cop, and that's a plus in my favor. I look around to get my bearings and find the streetlight I remember from last night, and work out in my head about where I parked the bus—and if I'm right, there's a car parked right in the same spot. So I go over and start hunkering down and looking through the gravel for anything glinting silver.

After digging out about twenty-five pull rings from beer cans, I move on to where I last seen Brian, lying in the gravel. Some of the gravel has been moved or swept away, probably by the swarm of cops for their collection of evidence. So if my ring had been lying anywhere around the body, it's a sure thing they got it now. I feel my face turning hot again, just thinking about it.

I try looking around for the place I first found Brian's parked truck, but there's so many cars parked tight in there that I can't see a thing. So I have to walk back and search the ground while I'm figuring the route I took when I drove the truck to where I backed it up to the bus. I search in the gravel, at first moving it with my feet, and then I get down on my hands and knees, the gravel biting into them through my jeans. All I find are cigarette butts and rings broke off from beer cans. I'm looking so hard I forget there might be somebody watching, and pretty soon some guy stumbles over and stands looking down at me.

"Hey," he says, leaning on the side of a pickup.

I ignore him and keep looking.

"*Hey*," he says.

I get up and face him. He's tall and thin with long, dirty hair, and a scar like a C on his forehead. He don't even look mean, he just looks stupid.

"What the hell do you want?" I snap.

He peers at me with bloodshot eyes under half-closed lids. "Hey, what're you doing down there? You lose something?"

"Ain't any of your business now, is it?" I ask him. "Leave me alone." I turn around and start walking back over the ground between where I figure the bus and the truck were last night. I see a glint off something on the ground as a car with its headlights on turns into the parking area, so I bend over and pick up another beer tab ring.

"Hey."

I wheel around. The drunk's been following close behind me.

"I used to collect them things, too," he says. "I got me a whole shoebox full of 'em."

I fold my arms and give him my most effective bug-off stare. But I guess he ain't in any shape to focus that well. He swipes a hand through his stringy hair and burps. I can smell the beer from where I'm standing. Beer and horse piss ain't a good combination. But that don't stop this guy. He's still talking.

"Now, don't ask me how many of them there are," he's saying, "'cause I don't know. One time I tried to count 'em, but I kept losing count every time I got to seven hundred and fifty-nine. It was so freakin' weird, man."

I throw the ring tab onto the ground at our feet and turn around again, taking up my search where I left off. The drunk just keeps following—I can hear his boots crunching on the gravel.

"Hey, you're a foxy looking chick, man. Wanna see my shoebox of beer tabs? I can drive you to my place if you want. I don't show 'em to just anybody. Hey—you hear what I'm saying?"

I wheel around again, thinking maybe I could kick him in the groin.

"Hey," I yell, and then I get an idea flying through my head so fast, it almost knocks me over, so I tone down the voice a little. "Hey, what's your name?"

"My name's Wendell. What's yours?"

"Rebecca. Say—you said you got your car here?"

"Yeah, it's right over there." He points to an old brown Pinto.

"Great, yeah, I see. Um—I need you to do me a favor, Wendell. I need you to drive me somewhere."

"*Far out*. Sure, I'll drive you anywhere you need to go, man."

"I need to go to the ladies' room first, and then I'll be right out. Okay?"

"I'll wait right here."

I smile and nod and walk casually up to the door of the bar and walk right in, then cut sharply to the left and into the restroom. I'm trying to think about what to do next when I glimpse my reflection in the foggy mirror hanging over the grimy sink. I look like a deranged woman, somebody I don't even recognize. My face is all twisted into a fearsome mask, and my hair is jutting out every which way, in almost the same shape I left Miz Stutts' in. I got dust from the gravel on my face and in my hair, and my eyes are all wild and bloodshot, almost as bad as Wendell's. My hands are shaking as I splash some cold water on my face and fish a comb out of my bag. I try to make myself look normal, but it don't help too much.

I wanna go on into the bar where I can look at the floor between the booth where Cindy and Becka and I were setting and the bar, and then over to the dance floor. If my ring fell off while I was dancing, it could have been kicked all over hell and half of Georgia. I don't know why I didn't think of that before. But at least it would mean the cops may not have found it, and it wouldn't necessarily connect the body and me. Hell, anybody could lose a ring dancing.

I open the door just a bit, and peer out to see if there might be any cops hanging around, but I don't see any. So I walk out and make a quick pass by the booth, kind of stooping to look under it as I go by, and then I retrace my route from last night, all the way to the bar, sweeping my eyes back and forth and scanning the corners and under the stools. Even though I feel conspicuous, as if everybody's eyeing me, and at any moment somebody's gonna remember me, turns out there's so many people crammed in here tonight, I don't think anybody's even noticed me at all. But I don't like to press my luck, so I head on back outside, just as two uniformed cops are swinging the door open to come inside. I turn my head to the side and slide on out, hoping they don't look at me. Then I head right for Wendell, who, true to his word, is still standing in the exact same spot.

"Hey, man," he says, grinning. "The cops are here. Wooowooowooo," He makes a siren sound and twirls his finger in the air, followed by his machine-gun laugh.

"Stop it. Let's go." I grab him by the arm, but he hangs back.

"Hey, relax, man." He's still laughing. "I think I gotta go too, now. It's all them beers—you know how they say you only rent 'em. I'll be right back."

He starts to head for the door but I pull him back, still hanging on to his arm. "No," I say. "I mean, I have to go *right now*. It's important."

He puts both hands up. "Hey, don't blow a gasket. All right, all right—hey . . ." He stops, rocking on his heels a little, and looks right at me like he ain't ever seen me before until right now. "Hey—I remember you . . ."

I look at him, confused. "Huh?"

"Sure, man, you're that girl last night. At the bar."

My heart does a leap. "No, I was at a movie last night. *Sting*—you know, Robert Redford. You saw somebody else. Now let's *go*."

"No, man, I may be dumb but I ain't stupid. I remember seeing you right here in this bar last night. Yeah—you was dancing and I was watching you from a barstool. And I was saying to myself, 'Now there's a far-out chick, real cute.' And then the bar closed down so we all had to leave, and I had to make a pit stop and then when I went outside I seen you setting in that VW bus with the window down, and I was gonna go up and talk to you, but you weren't alone. Yeah, I remember now. You were setting there with that guy—hey—you were setting in there with that dead guy, only—he wasn't dead yet. Far *out* . . ."

I slide my eyes sideways long enough to see one of them cops coming back outside, and he's looking all around. I turn to Wendell and shake both of his arms. "You gonna give me a ride, or not? Look, I'll pay you. I'll pay you a hundred dollars. Just think how many damn pull rings you can get with that."

But Wendell's looking at me real strange, his red eyes all wide. "I don't think so, man—I gotta go. Sorry, but I forgot about some stuff I gotta do." And he backs up into a parked car, then turns around and hightails it toward the bar.

So I hightail it too, in the other direction. There ain't no time to find a ride; I just gotta go. I dodge between the cars and pickups and I can't tell if the booming in my ears is the music coming from the bar or my heart. When I get to the other side of the building I glance back to see if anybody's coming around the corner yet, and then I break into a run, heading downhill for the beach.

I stop and take off my boots, carrying them as I run in the sand on the flat part next to the water, until I can't run no more and I stand there gasping for air with my hands on my knees and my head down. The wind has picked up and the spray hits my face. A laughing gull cackles down at me like it knows everything and I throw one of my boots at it, then pick it back up and start running again.

Running on the beach ain't any way to make headway, especially when you don't know where you're going. Where I want to go is home, but that's the first place they'll look when they find out who I am. I think about sneaking to the Beauty Barn and getting the bus, but they'll recognize it first thing, with their APBs and such. I watch plenty of TV; that old bus would stick out like a sore thumb—I might as well put a neon sign on the side of it that says *Here I am—come and get me.*

No, I just have to get away somewhere I can hunker down and think what I'm gonna do next. I gotta hide, and I gotta think. That's all I know. I look for a public beach entrance and tramp through the deeper sand up to the road again, and look around to try to figure out where I am now. The street sign says Beach Street and Magnolia Avenue, and I am amazed I've run so far. It's no wonder my legs ache and my head is pounding—I'm about into town.

It's dark now; the breeze off the water chills me in my sweaty clothes. I can still smell the perm solution and it makes my stomach turn as I walk away from the beach, going up Magnolia to Second Street. I'm looking for a place to sit and hide—anywhere where the cops won't see me if they pass by in their car. I go left down Second and turn right onto Frigate Street, and then walk down to Third.

I squint up Third, at what looks like a little alley, across the street and most of the way up the block, next to the pawnshop. I stand there on Frigate for a minute, watching and listening. There's very little traffic right now; I guess everybody's finishing up the dinner dishes and setting down to watch *All in the Family*. It makes me wish I was doing the same thing, though I hate doing dinner dishes and watching *All in the Family*. I'd sure as hell be happy doing it right now, though. Hell, I'd be ecstatic cleaning the toilets instead of this.

The other alleys I've passed are too damn wide and lit up with streetlights. I never realized there was so many damn streetlights in this town. No, that narrow place looks okay. I can rest there out of sight a while and maybe eventually find something to eat, if I dare. Maybe I'll find a way to call Cindy again or even Becka.

I turn onto Third but stop a little ways down, thinking I hear something. I duck real quick into the shadows of a building and flatten up against the brick. I can't see anything very clear in darkness all splotched by streetlights. The wind has died down, now that I'm away from the beach, and it's pretty still. Except for that noise. I listen, and make out low voices and a rustling, down the street. It seems to be coming from the narrow alleyway where I was heading, so I stand there and try to make out what's going on.

I can see shadows at the mouth of the alley, but nobody to make them. The voices are coming from the shadows, and I hear a high-pitched laugh that gives me the freaking heebie-jeebies, something like out of an asylum. I look around to see if I'm hidden okay. The nearest streetlight is far enough away from me that its light doesn't quite reach, so I guess I am.

I hear another voice, a lower, calmer one, and it sounds deliberate, like it's trying to explain something to somebody real slow. Then I hear that laugh again—that horrible laugh—and then muffled thumps and thuds like a fight is going on. Then there's a scuffle and suddenly dark shapes are coming out of the alley, three of them, and they're dragging something between them. At first I think it's a big bag, then I can see it has arms and legs dragging on the ground, and I know it's a man. Three men dragging another one. Then a couple more men come out of the alley, one moving slow. They dump the man at the mouth of the alley and I hear a couple of them talking fast, but I can't make out what they're saying.

Then one of the men hauls off and kicks the one on the ground real hard, again and again and again, and the other two join in, and I hear a moan that makes me sick to my stomach coming from the one lying on the ground. Every time they kick him it sounds like when my granny used to beat the rugs. She'd hang one of her thick rugs over the fence and beat the dust out of it with my father's old baseball bat over and over until every last speck of dust was purged out of it.

Them men just keep on kicking and kicking, their shadows doing a grotesque dance on the walls around them, until I can almost feel it myself. I want to scream, but I slap both hands over my mouth and close my eyes tight. I don't want to see this—I don't.

Finally the pummeling stops and the men just stand there looking down at the man on the ground, one of them talking again real low to the others. They look around, and I close my eyes so they won't see me. When I open my eyes, the three men are moving. At first I think they're coming my way, but I can see when they pass under a streetlight that they're walking down Third toward Magnolia, going the opposite way. I realize my hands are drawn up into fists, and I been holding my breath. I let it out real slow, feeling dizzy.

I stand there a long time, listening, shivering in a cold sweat, my heart still beating fast, but I don't hear nothing at all. Everything's as still as if nothing ever happened, but I can still see that dark shape on the ground beside the alley, and it's not moving.

Suddenly I see a shadow, small like an animal, coming out of the alley. It stops at the shape lying there, sniffing at it. I get the sick feeling it's a giant rat, gonna start eating the body, but after a while it crosses the street and then it starts to walk toward Frigate where the three men were going, but then it stops and comes back down Third toward me, moving real jerky-like. As it gets near me I can see it's a little dog that's got only three legs, and that's why it's moving funny. It's got red smeared on its head like it's been hurt, and it looks dazed, shaking its head some. Damn men probably kicked the dog, too.

It doesn't even look over at me as it passes by just a few feet away. It stops again, looking around bewildered, not making a noise, and then turns around and limps all the way back down Third the way it come. This time it just keeps going, on past the man, and on past Schooner Street, not looking one way or the other, but like it's being pulled toward something.

I look at the shape still lying there, and then down Third where them men disappeared, seeing if they might be coming back, but the street's empty. I decide

I gotta see if the man is alive or not. I wait a few more minutes, and there ain't even been one car pass by. So I try to stay in the shadows, and walk down the sidewalk, keeping an eye on the shape on the ground, trying not to let my boots click on the pavement. I keep moving past the buildings till I get across the street from the man, and I check down the street both ways again real good to make sure nobody's coming. Then I cross over and stand looking down at him.

I ain't ever seen a man beaten to a bloody pulp before, but I'm seeing it now. His dark face is so mauled I can't even tell where his eyes are—just two slits in a bloody mess. He's lying sprawled in an unnatural heap like somebody threw him from a building or something, and blood is trailing out his mouth onto the pavement. I stoop down and push him gently on the shoulder, but he's limp as a doll. There's a dark stain around his crotch and it smells like he shit himself. I stare at his chest to see if he's breathing, but there's no movement, so I put my hand down flat on it, and it feels like there's something broke inside. I snatch my hand back and catch my breath.

"*Shit, oh shit oh shit,*" I hear myself saying, kind of half crying like a kitten mewling. Then I stand and move to the wall and lose anything that ever thought about being my dinner.

One time when I was real little, I saw a dog get hit by a car. It wasn't chasing it or nothing, it just wanted to cross the street, and some damn car came around the corner and hit it good. The dog bounced off the tires and the car just kept going, leaving the dog lying broken and bleeding in the street. It all happened so fast I didn't have time to blink. I remember I didn't want to see it lying there, but I couldn't take my eyes off it. And then my mama called me in for supper and I didn't have no choice but to go inside.

I was too upset; I couldn't talk about it. At dinner I just moved the food around on my plate, so Mama thought I was sick and sent me to bed. Later on, lying in bed in the dark, I felt bad—guilty, I guess, for just leaving it there in the street. But I was little and didn't know what to do. I remember I fell asleep crying into the pillow so nobody'd hear me, my tears making the pillow all soggy wet. The next morning, first thing, I ran downstairs and out the front door and down the street to where the dog had been lying, but it was gone—the blood and everything. And I wondered if I'd dreamed it.

Now I sink down to the ground and the tears come streaming down my face, and I can't stop them. I set there sobbing like a four-year-old, something I ain't done in so long, I can't remember. At first I think I'm crying for the broken man, but after a while I don't know anymore. I think maybe I'm crying because I don't know what else to do. I just want my Mama to put me to bed.

Soon I hear footsteps coming this way fast from Schooner Street, and I panic and get up and run the other way, turning right onto Magnolia and heading back down toward the beach like I'm running for my frigging life.

6

Willie

When Sera leaves to go take care of her business, I know it's time Goblin and I got to go take care of ours, so we crawl out of the Palace and I peek around the corner and look around both ways real good to make sure there ain't any aliens lying in wait. It looks all clear, so he and I head on off for the porta john we seen at a vacant lot on Frigate near Beach Road, where they're gonna be building a new house. It's a real luxury for me, so I take full advantage of it. When I got to take care of business, sometimes I go down to the gas station 'cause they usually keep it unlocked, and sometimes I just gotta do the best I can.

After we take care of that, I got the added luxury of not having to find something to eat, 'cause that big cheeseburger is taking up all the room I got and more. Goblin looks like he's feeling pretty good and wants to walk, though, so I decide we can head on down to where the fishing boats come in and see what we can see.

I don't know what I would do if I couldn't live near the water like I do. I always liked being near a body of water, even if it was only the little pond down the road from the house I lived in when I was a boy. I spent a lot of time there, swimming and fishing and just sitting and thinking and watching the clouds float by like big white sails on a blue-water sky. And though that was a long time ago, sometimes even now, when my mind's eye is clear, I'll get a sense of being there still that comes on me quick—maybe from a certain smell in the springtime that reminds me of the wildflowers that grew around the pond, or the way the summer sun glints off the water when it's calm, or even the sound and feel of the warm water when I dip my hand in it—that takes me right back through all them years like flipping pages in a book.

There's something about the water I can't describe, something fine that fills up an empty space in me, almost like something spiritual. There's big chunks of time goes by, I don't even know what month it is, only if it's too cold or too hot or somewhere in between. But in the early spring, when the flower buds are peeking out and the sun shines a little warmer on my face, folks come to this little town from all over to watch the Blessing of the Fleet, and then I know it must be Palm Sunday.

Through the years I've learned they started the Blessing somewhere else in the world, and now we got our own right here. It was supposed to be for the fishermen, but now anybody who got a boat can bring it up the Cape Fear River and get a blessing from the chaplain standing on the stern of a boat named *Called to See*. All kinds of boats come through to be blessed for fair weather and a safe season—little tiny boats that look like canoes all the way up to shrimp boats and fancy yachts. One time, a huge container ship come through, but it was just too big to get in line, so it went on out to sea, the chaplain waving a blessing after it the best he could.

Folks are welcome to gather around on the shore and the pier and watch, but I stand back out of folks' way, so I can't hear too well. They got their dogs on leashes and the little kids hold crusts of bread up for the gulls to grab. Then, to start things, somebody lights the town cannon and it goes off with a loud boom, can be heard for miles. It's enough to make you jump out of your shoes if you ain't expecting it. Then the chaplain out on his boat commences saying words over all those people as the line of boats passes by.

I guess it makes them feel safe, kind of like when Mama and Papa and all us kids went every Sunday to hear the Reverend Blythe. His voice was deep and velvet smooth when he delivered his sermon; sometimes he'd talk quiet and low, and folks would lean up in their seats, the women fanning themselves with their programs. Then he'd pound on the podium, a big vein sticking out in the middle of his forehead and his voice booming out like thunder and bouncing off the walls, till them same folks would be slumping in their seats like they was sure some lightning gonna come down and strike them dead any minute.

Of course I didn't understand all those words when I was little, but I liked the *sound* of them, the way they got into my head—the way I like the sound of the water washing over the sand. Now that I'm a man, I think about some of the words I do remember, although they're mostly from hymns. It makes me feel like there's something good always gonna be there, something constant—even for an old bum like me. As a matter of fact, I been thinking on the spiritual side a lot lately. Why, I couldn't tell you.

Now I walk down toward the inlet where the shrimp boats and fishing boats come in in the late afternoon and evening to anchor out in the water for the night. Goblin and I walk along the beach, careful to stay out of anybody's way, although there ain't but a few people around this part of the strand 'cause there's too many rocks out in the water to swim or wade. We sit ourselves down and watch the sun move across the sky for a long time, listening to the black-hooded laughing gulls and big speckled herring gulls fussing over bits of food. Once in a while there's a long string of pelicans flying low over the water, barely flapping, just mostly gliding along, looking like them big dinosaur birds or something. When Goblin sees them he drops open his mouth and pants like he's laughing. I think he wants to join them.

We sit there most of the afternoon 'cause it's so pleasant and there ain't no one to bother us, and we ain't bothering no one. Then when the sun gets way behind us in the west and shadows from the sea oats on the dunes are growing long and snaky across the sand, Goblin and I make our way down near the water and settle down again. There's already a few boats dropped their anchors, starting to make ready for the night, lights on down in their cabins, little flags on the decks snapping in the breeze. The sky is dark gray with an orange glow to it, and the wind dies down just a little. I like this time of day by the water—the sight of it, the sounds of it, the pull of it.

Long time ago when I was younger and had more courage, I talked to some fishermen, come back from a stormy bad day at sea; I asked them why it was they do what they do. One of them said it gives a man a new way to look at things, since everything's always changing out there, from one day to the next. One told me he don't like working around too many people—he likes the solitude. And one young fella said the sea seems to want a part of us back, always reaching out like it does—and that for him the pull is so strong he just can't resist it.

Some men feel that pull more than others. That's why them fishermen go out early every morning and stay out to sea for days at a time—it ain't just the fish, you see, makes some of them do it. It's the pull they feel. If there weren't any fish, they'd have to find another reason to go.

It's an honorable way to make a living, being a fisherman, but it's a hard way to live. You can tell by looking at a fisherman's face, all lined deep from the sun and salt wind and hard work. And it's a danger, too, going out on that water—no land in sight, the sky going on and on so high over you and the ocean going on and on so deep under you, and the little boat you're on suspended in the middle of it, the only thing keeping you safe, till you begin to think about how small a thing you really are in all the Lord's creation.

I know there's different things pull people different ways, some good and some bad. In my life I been pulled by my voices till they almost pulled me apart. Sometimes I'm amazed old Willie's still here.

Then there's others who feel the kind of pull, makes them want to understand things and see what makes them tick. I think of Miss Sera and how she's like that, hungry for pieces of the puzzle, gonna show her just who she is and what she wants. Oh, deep down inside she knows what she wants, all right, but *she* don't think she does. When a child don't have a mama and her daddy don't care, that child gonna grow up, all right, but it's likely when she do, her sense of self gonna be just like a lump of clay—ain't been molded into some kind of shape yet—and that young woman ain't gonna know what to do with herself. It ain't her fault, but she might feel like it is.

I don't think Sera's gonna find anything in that Lissa girl that she ain't already got enough of herself if she were to look real hard, but I can see she's bent on looking for them puzzle pieces, and she's come an awful long way to do just that. No matter what she seems like, that girl got a stubborn streak in her, I can tell.

I had a sister named Sarah, only one year older than me. She was the most mule-headed person ever walked on this earth. If Papa told her to feed the chickens, she'd light off and disappear till one of us other kids done it instead. If Mama told her to go put on her nice, clean, freshly pressed blue dress to go to Sunday Meeting, she'd come skipping outside in the dirty, wrinkled red one she'd had her heart set on wearing instead. Mama would tell her, 'Now girl, you take yourself right back inside and change,' but Sarah would put up such a fuss, till we'd be late for church and have to find places to sit in the folding chairs set up in the back row meant for the late sinners. That vein in Reverend Blythe's head would already be sticking out, and him already halfway into his thunder.

Mama would cut a switch soon as we got home from church, but Sarah was too obstinate even to cry. Who could have known that someday all that pigheadedness would turn out to be useful when she got herself a scholarship to go off to college and become a successful lawyer?

Sera ain't that bad, but sure enough, I can see the same spark of it in her deep down, and I know for a fact, once she grabs onto something she thinks is important, she ain't gonna let it go easy, and that's for sure. You can take that right on down to the bank.

It makes me feel good to be around a young person like her; seems like all her wants and dreams are so fresh and new and unspoiled, at least, compared to me. Her skin is smooth and fresh, too. If I was a young man her age, I might think about what it would be like to kiss her. But thoughts like that aren't for old Willie.

Then I think, maybe if things had been different and I'd married Iris and the two of us had a daughter, she would be something like Sera. Thinking like that gives me a strange feeling inside, like I want to protect her from the bad things I've seen, and I can only hope she's careful while she's in this world with us.

After a while it gets so dark my old eyes have trouble seeing much, and Goblin, lying beside me in the sand, looks ready to get back. In fact, judging by the way the stars are shining faintly through the clouds over the dark water, and how the lights have gone off inside the boats so they're just dark shapes in the water, I think he and I might have nodded off for a time. So we get ourselves up and brush off the sand and stretch out our stiff muscles some, and walk back down the beach a while to where we can take the access path that cuts through to Beach Road. Even though I used to do it all the time, I ain't walked around this late for a long time. It feels so good, I don't remember why.

Everything's quiet; when we pass by some houses, they only have maybe one or two windows lit up, like the folks inside them are watching the news or getting ready for bed. It's a lonely time of day, but ever since Goblin came around I don't get an ache from it like I did, and my step is a little lighter, too.

We walk all the way down till we get to Magnolia, and then go up to Third and home to the Palace. By then we're glad to be home after such a walk. There ain't no porch light on to greet us, but we're used to that. We just turn right on into the alley and crawl inside without thinking much about nothing. My good luck shells click together and the smell of onions from that big old cheeseburger still hangs in the air. But even though it's been hours since we ate, my stomach still feels full.

I take a last swig of my arthritis medicine and Goblin settles down in his corner. I tell him, "Now, ain't it just been the *best* kind of day," and he thumps his tail once, blinking his tired eyes at me in full agreement.

That good little walk made me tired and I fall asleep almost as soon as I lie down and get myself settled in, listening to the sound of the surf coming from what seems to be far away, now that we're back home.

I don't know how long I been asleep before Goblin's stirring all around acting fitful, sitting up with his nose in the air like he's smelling something. I raise my head up but I don't smell nothing but them onions, and I don't hear nothing, either. So I tell him, "Go on and lie back down, now, and go to sleep."

Well, he looks at me and then at the rag door, and gets up and walks over to it, and stands there with his ears at attention, not moving a muscle.

I'm just sitting up myself when all of a sudden, I hear a loud *pop* come down from the ceiling of the box, and then another *pop*, and I look up and see something hanging down from the middle of the ceiling, looks like two big knife blades. I barely got time to blink before them blades start sawing their way through the cardboard, both of them moving outward from the middle, cutting through the strings so my shells are falling all around me, the luck gone out of them.

The knives don't stop when they get to the sides; they just saw down through them, the blades hollering and squeaking through the cardboard till my ears ring and Goblin sits trembling in his corner again, him and me not knowing where to go because them blades are tearing the Palace in two.

It comes to me to grab for my bottle to use as a weapon, but just then the sides of the box cave in on me and I'm being pulled out of it like a rag doll. It's dark in the alley, but I see them same aliens that attacked me back in March. Now they're standing in front of me and behind me, the brick walls closing in the sides. The alien rat kid with long, stringy hair is standing right in front of me, grinning with those yellow teeth of his. I wonder, since he's an alien who got the power to change how he look, why he'd wanna look like that.

"Well, well, well," he says to me. "If it ain't our crazy old friend the tramp-in-a-box—*ooops*—only now it looks like he ain't got no box, so he's just a plain ole tramp. Ain't that right, y'all?"

The stocky looking alien behind him starts that high laughing that cuts through me like one of them knife blades they used to cut up the Palace. The others in the alley behind me start chuckling along. But out of the corner of my good eye I see little Goblin coming out from what's left of the cardboard ruins. What I want to do is tell him to run, but instead I try to keep the aliens' attention on myself so maybe they won't know he's there.

So I say, "Now, why don't you all just go on back to your ship and fly out of here back to where you're truly appreciated? We don't want no trouble here on this planet. We got enough as it is."

That awful laughing starts up again, and the rat kid draws up near to my face till I can smell the stink of his breath. "It wasn't very nice of you to move without sending us a card, now, was it? You thought we wouldn't find you here, is that it, old man? As I recall, you weren't a very good host last time, so I had to make you a promise, crazy man—you remember what it was?"

I shake my head.

"Well, I do. I remember real well, just like it was fuckin' yesterday."

Now I look at him dead in the eye, because for a moment he sounds just like the demon voice Jake from long ago, and I think, *How can that be?* I'm looking at that punk alien rat kid but it's a demon's voice coming out of his mouth instead.

"I told you one day something bad was gonna happen to you, didn't I?" he says to me. "*Didn't I*, crazy man. And I always make good on a promise."

He's still grinning as he draws back a fist. I grab his arm, but the big one behind him moves forward like a flash and hits me square in the eye. I fall back against the ones behind me, and they stand me up again.

Now Goblin runs straight at the one that hit me and clamps his jaws down hard on that alien's leg. He holds on for dear life while the alien jumps back in pain and then tries shaking him off, cussing and yelling, "Get him off me!"

One of the others hauls off and kicks that little dog hard right in the head, stunning him so he lets go, and then he kicks him again so powerful that Goblin just crumples and lies there like he's dead, and I'm thinking he probably is.

I don't care what they do to me no more. I run at the one kicked Goblin and shove him into the brick wall with all my weight, knocking his thick head against it with a thud. He goes down, and then all hell breaks loose. I don't know which one is which anymore, I just know one of them hits me square in the face again and I must have passed out for a second, 'cause the next thing I know, I'm being dragged out of the alley onto the sidewalk.

They lay me out where there's more room and then I see the pointy boots of the rat kid beside me, and them boots start to wallop me and kick me all over—in my sides and my legs and my shoulders—and he's moving around me like he's doing a dance. One of them boots comes out and kicks me in the head; it feels like a railroad spike driven into my skull. Everything goes black except for tiny little stars moving around inside my eyelids, and I pray he'll stop. But he keeps doing it over and over and over, and then there's more boots kicking at me, and the pain's so bad . . . I hear somebody moaning; it doesn't sound like me, but it must be me: "Please Lord, let me die . . ."

Then, all of a sudden, I feel myself floating up from the ground and hovering over it somewhere, looking down at the aliens kicking and kicking some other man. I'm looking down thinking to myself, *Why they doing that to that old man? Why?*

Then everything goes a soft fuzzy gray and I can't see or hear nothing at all no more.

But there's a fishing boat floating far out to sea—the endless sky towering high above it, the great Atlantic Ocean stretching deep down below, and that boat suspended somewhere in the middle, rocking gently with the waves. I lie there on the boat and all my eyes can see is the gray fog, but inside my head I see what look like old movies of things, one right after another.

I see my Mama smiling in her bright yellow Sunday Meeting dress, a daisy one of us kids picked—white with a bright yellow center—stuck in the band of her big floppy hat. Papa's there too, and he looks down at me and puts one of his big warm hands on my head like he used to, sometimes. I see that vacant lot by the drugstore and the neighbor kid Elijah Smith knocking a homer right over our heads. I see all us kids piling into Papa's old Model A Ford to go for ice cream on a hot summer day.

Then I see my big sister Mary, and she's standing in the snow looking at me, trying to say something, but I can't hear her and I can't make out the words.

7

Sera

8:55 p.m.

When Gabe comes back into the living room, he's back in his old jeans and a worn blue tee shirt. It's taken a long time for him to change. I wonder how he manages by himself.

"If I wasn't stuck in this chair, I'd go looking for her," he says, still sounding frustrated. "But we don't even have the bus."

"Where do you suppose Lissa might be, this time of evening?" I wonder out loud.

He shakes his head. "I don't know. Last night she went out. She was at the Riverview Bar with two of her friends—at least, that's what she told me."

"Can you try calling her friends?"

Gabe sighs and lifts the receiver, checking a small book next to the phone for the numbers. He dials one, then the other, and finally puts the receiver down. "No luck. Nobody's home. Becka works at the hospital, so she could be working a late shift—I don't know. And Cindy? That girl could be anywhere." Gabe rubs his eyes. "To be honest, I think Lissa could be out with another man. I don't want to think it, but I've seen all the signs."

I slide toward him on the sofa. "Gabe, you don't know that. She's only a few hours late. There's probably a good explanation."

He looks at me. "You're a good person, Sera. You might as well go home. All I can do now is be here and wait for her. There's no need for you to sit here listening to me. It's getting late."

I don't tell him what I really think—that Lissa might be in some kind of trouble, that it could be a precursor to something far worse, and that I need to find her. Instead I say, "I could go out and look for her myself, if you're worried. I could at least go to the beauty shop and maybe check out the bar, look for the bus. Then at least you would know she's okay."

Gabe shakes his head. "That would be way too far to walk, especially in the dark. We may look like a little old innocent town, but we've got crime here just like anywhere else." He looks at me, concern in his eyes. "Don't you have a car?"

"Well, no—it's being fixed," I tell him. I'm getting tired of lying to this man.

"But how will you get home in the dark? It's late."

I smile at him. It feels rather good to have someone concerned about me. "Don't worry about me. I can call someone. Isn't there some kind of driving service?"

Gabe looks blank for a moment. "You mean a taxi? Sure, but they charge an arm and a leg."

"It's fine. I'll call one and use it to look around town for a while. Don't worry about the money—I'm certainly not."

"No way; I can't ask you to do this. You've done too much already, and I can't even pay you today."

I touch the arm of his chair. "Look, Gabe." I look right into his clear blue eyes. "You won't understand this, but you've done more for me in one afternoon than anyone else in my whole life. You've welcomed me into your home and made me feel like a part of the family. You'll never know how much that means to me. And if I can help out by making sure Lissa's okay right now, it's the least I can do. Besides, she'll probably show up any minute. I'm sure of it."

Somehow I don't believe my last words ring true for either of us.

Gabe looks down at the arm of his chair where my hand is lightly resting, a curious, almost startled look on his face. He hesitantly puts his hand over mine. "Like I said before," he says, "you're a special person."

Our eyes lock, and I feel so strongly drawn to this man that my heart skips a beat. I can almost feel his deep blue eyes trying to penetrate my façade. All I know is that they seem filled with the same hunger I feel inside. He leans forward, reaches up, and gently caresses my cheek—his touch so electric I can't help but draw a sharp, surprised breath.

"Who are you, Sera?" he asks. "Who are you, really?"

I want to tell him who I really am and why I'm here. I want to tell him that Lissa and I are one and the same entity, only from different times and two different worlds. I want to tell him that more than anything, I want to stay right here and never go back, and learn how to make tuna fish salad, and play outside in the afternoon sun with Hailey and Bug. I want to sit right here with him on long quiet evenings while we hold each other close.

But I can't.

I'm aware of the surf pounding just down the hill from us—it seems to grow louder, resounding inside my head, merging with the blood coursing through my veins, working its way into my psyche as some ancient, insatiable force I have never before encountered. I have never felt this way before.

I reach up and touch the contour of his jaw, his lightly tanned face warm and strong under my fingers. I can smell the aftershave he used and the underlying male musk of his body. My face feels flushed; my lips part, but I can't speak. He closes his eyes as though he feels the same electricity as I. He gently puts a hand on either side of my face and pulls me toward his own, until our lips meet and I close my eyes, breathless, my heart beating fast, lost in him. For now, nothing else exists in any place or any time—it's just the two of us right here, right now.

Then Bug's voice comes from the room down the hall. "Mama."

Gabe slowly withdraws his hands from my face and sits back. My heart is beating fiercely and I take a deep breath. Our moment has passed.

"I'll go," I say to him, my voice shaky, "if you think it would be all right."

He nods and smiles.

When I open the door, Bug is sitting up in bed. Hailey is curled up asleep in her own bed, thumb in mouth. I look at Bug and hold a finger to my lips. "Shh."

He rubs his eyes. "Mama?" he says, and I realize he thinks I'm Lissa in the dark. For a moment I think so, too.

"It's Sera, Bug," I whisper. "What's wrong?"

"I'm *scared*, Sewa."

"Of what, Bug?"

"Da boogie man."

"There's not any boogie man, Bug. You're safe."

He rubs his eyes and blinks at me, still not convinced. "I'm thoosty, Sewa. I want some wadew."

"Sure, I'll get you some. Be right back, okay?"

"Okay."

I get a little cup of water from the bathroom across the hall and hand it to him. He drinks noisily, slurping until it's all gone, and holds out the cup, out of breath. "Moah?"

I get him more and he drinks it all down and wipes his mouth with his arm, then looks up at me. "Whew's Mama?"

I push his hair out of his face. "She's not home yet, but I'm sure she'll be back real soon. You okay now?"

Bug scrunches up his face; I can see it in the faint light from the bathroom. "I want *Mama*."

I put my arm around him and give him a hug; although he's three, I can still smell his clean baby smell. "I'll just bet that if you go to sleep right now, you'll see her in the morning when you wake up."

He sits there in the semidarkness, his baby fine hair sweaty and sticking up where he was lying on it, his sleepy eyes half closed, looking at me. Then he nods, and lies back down. "Den can you sit on da bed wif me?"

"I'll stay right here until you fall asleep. I promise."

"Nightie night." He closes his eyes. For a while he peeks to make sure I'm still there, and then his breathing becomes slow and regular.

"Nightie night, Bug," I whisper.

When I close the door, I have to lean against the wall for a minute. I close my eyes and put a hand to my mouth; I can still almost feel Gabe's lips on mine. There are too many emotions stirred up inside me all at once—it's too hard to keep them captive. I know I must leave quickly and find Lissa James. The short time I have here is passing and all I've accomplished is falling in love with her family so completely that I have become almost incapacitated where my original goals are concerned.

For a moment I have to remind myself what they were: to observe my past entity and discover the reason for her death, so I can arrive at some kind of peace within my own life. I shake my head. Now it seems rather selfish and cold. Willie was right—whatever happens, how will I resolve the passive role I must play in her death? Or the severe longing I now have to take over her life? Will these things play against each other somehow?

When I walk into the living room, Gabe puts down the phone. "They're sending a taxi for you. It'll be about fifteen minutes."

I nod and we avoid each other's eyes for a minute.

"Bug was thirsty and wanted his Mama," I tell him. "He's okay now."

Gabe looks at me. "Look, I'm sorry about that. I don't know what to say, except I hope all this won't put you off. I hope that after all this is over, you'll stay—come back once in a while, I mean, for Hailey and Bug's sakes. I promise I'll be good."

"You don't have to apologize, Gabe," I tell him. "Everything's okay."

But he and I both know it isn't.

We sit quietly, waiting for the taxi, each lost in our own thoughts, afraid to say them out loud. At my request, Gabe writes down the addresses of the beauty parlor and the bar, and their own phone number, in case I find Lissa, on a piece of paper. When he folds it and gives it to me, his hand is shaking a little. Then all too soon the horn sounds outside, two quick bursts, and I rise to leave. Gabe smiles and puts up a hand.

"I'll call you later," I tell him, and run out to the car before I can change my mind.

9:58 p.m.

The driver is a small, stocky man in his fifties, sweaty and balding, his white shirtsleeves rolled up and dark stains under his arms. He wears a gold chain around his thick neck and his flabby jaws persistently work up and down, chewing a wad of gum. I show him the addresses and he nods without asking any questions, for which I'm grateful.

As we leave, I can't help looking back. Who would have thought that the rusty, old trailer sitting in the dark with faint light seeping through its small, square windows could contain my whole world?

The streets are dark and still, only an occasional set of headlights breaking into my thoughts. I look up at the driver's picture ID, displayed on the dash along with the meter. *Curtis O'Neal*, it says.

"Mr. O'Neal?"

His eyes flash at me in the rearview mirror. "Call me Curtis, will you? Mr. O'Neal makes me feel old."

"I'm looking for a certain Volkswagen bus at those two addresses. But I might need you to drive me a to couple more places. I hope that's okay."

He looks at me in the rearview mirror. "It's your money." He turns on the radio; the news is on, but he turns the knob, moving through the stations until he finds some light jazz. "Okay with you?" he asks.

"Fine," I say, not caring.

It takes a few minutes to get to the beauty parlor on the other side of town. Even though it has a small-town feel, Port William is larger and more spread out than I had originally thought. We turn into a line of shops and stop in front of one at the end. The sign over it is dark, but the letters painted in white on the window identify it as the Beauty Barn.

Curtis nods toward it, snapping his gum. "The wife comes here sometimes."

I get out of the car and try to look through the windows, but the shades are pulled down over them and over the window in the door. A sign hanging on the door says *Closed*, and the door is locked when I try it. I walk around the corner of the building to the side parking lot.

There is the bus, parked in the first slot. I walk over to it and touch the hood; it's cool. The doors are locked, the keys gone. I look around but there's no sign of anyone at all, only the soft sound of jazz coming from the taxi. I have a sinking feeling in my gut.

Where are you, Lissa? I say to the dark bus.

The taxi moves through the streets again; we drive into a different part of town where the number of houses and shops dwindles. I see a high bridge spanning what looks like a wide river far below. There are a few lights, but I can't tell if they're from small boats or maybe from piers jutting out into the black water.

I look up through the window at a sky that is a deep, velvet black, with stars sprinkled over it, shimmering like fairy dust. I have never seen a sky like this before in the city, where there are always lights. The stars are beautiful, and it's hard to take my eyes off them.

Soon we turn off the main road onto another, narrower one that winds around and down. If it was dark before, it's inky here. In the distance, a small building sits lit up, its red neon sign announcing *Riverview Bar*. Cars and trucks line its parking lot, lit by a faint yellow streetlight. We turn into the gravel lot and Curtis pulls up to the door.

"What you want to do, young lady?" he asks me.

I sit back and look around for a minute. People are coming out the double doors of the main entrance, and music blasts from behind them. "I'm going in. Wait for me, please?"

"Sure thing. I'll have to park over there." He points to an open spot.

"I won't be long."

"Take your time. Like I said, it's your money."

I get out and walk inside. I have been in bars at home, but this one has a different flavor to it. The first thing I notice is the thick smoke hanging in the air, making it hard to breathe. The music is more rhythmic and primal, and people move to it in one corner of the big hazy room, dancing with an innate ease. The combined noise of the music and the crowd is deafening. I walk through the wall of people searching their faces, hoping to find Lissa among them.

A man with gold chains around his neck and the first four buttons of his shirt open to reveal thick, black chest hair moves in front of me and holds up a glass. "Let me buy you a beer, baby doll." I shake my head and skirt quickly by him, my eyes watering from the smoke.

I complete my circuit without seeing Lissa. A man in a uniform I take to be a policeman stands at the bar, listening to a younger, gaunter man with dirty, oily, long hair and a scar on his forehead. The younger man is supplementing his speech with his hands, occasionally pointing toward the door. I move nearer, pretending to look for someone.

"*Then* she tells me she's gonna give me a hundred dollars to drive her somewheres. A hundred bucks is a lot of money," the gaunt one's saying, his eyes red and watery. "Then you shoulda seen the look on her face when you pi—uh, policemen—came out looking around. You wanna know what I think? I think she killed that dude that was with her last night, and she come around tonight looking for *another* one. Foxy chick like her'll fool you every time. When she seen you, she lit out, running toward the beach." He shakes his head. "Never thought I'd be glad to see the fuzz. That bitch is *nuts*, man. Probably woulda cut my throat."

The policeman writes in a little notebook, nodding. "Just give me your name and address," he says calmly.

I back away and head out the door. Somehow I know they've got to be talking about Lissa. Something happened when she was here last night, something bad. And she's in some kind of trouble, all right; she's alone and on the run.

When I get outside I look down the road toward the beach. I can just make out the line of the water, illuminated by the faint light from a thin moon. There's no way I can find her down there while it's so dark, much less get that close to the ocean. I have to hope she came back up from the beach, somewhere farther into town. She might even be on her way back to the trailer.

Curtis is patiently waiting for me, his elbow resting on the sill of the open window, still wildly chewing his gum. "Okay?" he says.

"I need to ride into town," I tell him, getting in quickly.

"Okay." He starts the car and maneuvers it out of the parking space, avoiding a loud group of young women heading toward the bar. "Whereabouts we going?" he asks as he pulls onto the road.

"Just head toward town, and stay near the beach."

We turn back onto the main road and pass over the bridge again, and I wish it was light so I could see down to the river. I can't tell if it meets the ocean or if it winds along parallel with it. After a few minutes more we come into town again, with its houses and stores and streetlights. Curtis turns off the highway onto Coral Avenue, and then turns onto Mast.

"Slow down, please—and could you turn off the radio?"

Curtis obliges me. He even stops snapping his gum. "What're we looking for?" he finally asks.

"A girl. She's running around out here somewhere, lost and scared. I need to find her and bring her home."

"Oh, one of them," he says. "I got a daughter myself. You're a good friend, to look for her like this."

"Yeah, a real good friend." I feel a stab of guilt.

We move slowly down Mast, parallel with the water, and turn down Gull Street. He's making the circuit, slowly closing in to the water. So far I've only seen a group of rough-looking guys swaggering down Gull, heading away from town. I shudder to think Lissa may be out here somewhere near them, alone. Then, as we turn onto Third, I see something moving down the street.

"*Stop*," I say quickly. Curtis pulls over and stops the car. "Turn it off," I tell him.

We sit there and I stare at the thing coming down the street, still too far away for me to make it out. Something about it makes my heart leap into my throat—the way it moves. Finally it passes under a streetlight and I grab the door handle. "*Goblin*—it's Willie's dog."

Curtis cranes to see. "I don't see nothing."

"Right there. That little dog. Stay here and wait for me, please."

I get out and walk slowly toward the dog, watching his small shape in the fog that has sprung up. He's still a block away, and now he sees me and stops. I have a sick feeling in my stomach. Goblin never leaves Willie's side, ever. But now here he is, alone.

"Goblin—come here, boy. It's *me*. Remember me?"

The little dog starts as though he's terrified, and I'm afraid he'll run from me.

"Where's Willie, boy? *Where's Willie?*"

He stands there, looking around as though confused, and then he sits down where he is. I begin walking toward him again, slow and easy, talking to him all the way. When I get to him I can see he's been hurt. There's blood on his nose and I can see pain in his eyes. I kneel down and touch his head as I saw Willie do, and he closes his eyes as if he might recognize me after all.

I look back down the street and realize this is Willie's street, and that on down a few blocks is the alley with his Palace. I get up and start walking, completely forgetting about the taxi. Then I notice the little dog behind me, trying to keep up, but limping even more badly than before, so I turn and scoop him up gently and hurry on, hugging him to me so he won't be too badly jostled.

My legs are aching by the time I pass Frigate and come within sight of Willie's block of Third Street. Suddenly Goblin wiggles in my arms and struggles to get down, so I set him down and he limps quickly toward the alley, and straight to a dark heap on the sidewalk next to it. I stop short, my mouth falling open, my heart pumping hard with the sudden realization of what I'm seeing.

"*Willie*," I scream, and run to him. I fall to my knees beside him, not wanting to recognize that this poor, disfigured wretch lying in a pool of blood is really the charming, gentle man I met today. But I know his clothes, and I begin to cry. I touch his head and his arm, but there is no sign of life. "Willie, *no*," I hear myself saying over and over. Goblin lies down next to Willie, his body as close as possible, as though to keep it warm, and lays his head on his paw.

I glance over to the alley. I can see by the streetlight that the Palace is destroyed. Cardboard is scattered about; broken shells and rags are strewn everywhere.

Then I hear a low sound beside me, and I look up to see Curtis pulling up in his taxi, eyes open wide as he sees the man lying on the sidewalk beside me. Goblin gets up painfully and runs off down Third, faster than I would have thought possible. I look after him, wondering what will become of him now.

"Holy Mother of God," Curtis is saying as he slowly gets out of the car. "What happened to *him?*"

I look up at him, still sobbing. "We've got to get him to the hospital," I manage to say.

Curtis looks at Willie and then at his taxi, no doubt thinking about the blood.

"*I'll pay for the damage,*" I say through clenched teeth.

But he shakes his head. "Don't worry about it, young lady. Let's go."

We manage between the two of us to get Willie stretched out in the backseat of the taxi, and I ride back there with him, his swollen head cradled in my lap. As we drive through the streets, I look down at him. I have known this man for only a few hours, yet he is so dear to me. How can that be? How can someone go through an entire lifetime not having known such closeness, and finally find it, only to have it snatched away again? I feel the weight of all that has transpired today, and I cannot stop crying.

Curtis sits silent at the wheel, driving fast through the silent streets of Port William, no doubt wondering at the outlandish occurrences during his evening fare.

Curtis calls ahead on his radio, and when we arrive at the emergency room, a stretcher is ready for us. The men in white uniforms efficiently remove Willie from the taxi and put him on the narrow wheeled platform, buckle him in, and whisk him inside through double glass doors that open on their own. It's strange, but I am surprised that such technology exists in the twentieth century, and I think maybe I don't know anything at all.

One of the men dressed in white remains behind. "Where are they taking him?" I ask him, tears still drying on my face.

"ER. They'll do everything they can for him, Miss. Who is responsible for the man?"

I know they want to know how they will be paid. "I am responsible for him. Is he alive?"

The man in white shakes his head. "We'll have to wait," he says. "You can go on inside and fill out the papers, and they'll let you know how he is as soon as possible."

I look at Curtis. He's forgotten about his gum, and he stands with his hands in his pockets beside his taxi. I walk over to him and give him a hug. "Thank you so much for everything."

He blushes and looks away. "Glad I could help, young lady. I hope your friend makes it. And good luck with the young runaway, too. I can see you got your hands full."

My eyes fill again but I smile at him. I dig in my bag and bring out a hundred-dollar bill—from what I understand, it's a lot of money. I stuff it into his hand. "Is this enough?"

He gives it back to me. "I ain't taking this," he says. "My dear old Ma would slap me senseless from the Great Beyond if I did. You keep it, and think of Curtis sometimes. Okay?"

I smile at him through my tears and he smiles back, then gets in his taxi and drives away.

The lobby is well lit and nearly empty—only one couple is sitting in the chairs, besides me. A woman gives me some papers on a clipboard to fill out, and I do the best I can, although I have no way of knowing Willie's medical history. I have to leave much of it blank. For his address I put my own, which doesn't even exist yet. But I don't know what else to do.

When I give it back to the woman at the desk, she shakes her head, looking skeptical. "He doesn't have any insurance?"

"I put my name down for payment. I'm responsible."

She looks up. "Do you have some ID with you?"

I blink—I *am* my own ID. But not here. "I have money." I open my purse to show her.

The woman shakes her head again. "I don't think you realize what you're doing," she says. "It will probably be more than you think."

I lean toward her and look into her eyes. "I told you I have it covered," I say again.

She sighs and rolls her eyes and slips a paper clip onto the stack of papers. "You can have a seat right over there," she says abruptly, and turns her back to dig into her file cabinet.

I sit in a chair in the lobby and rest my head on my hand. A small television is on in the far corner of the large room, and the couple sits near it, transfixed. Soon I find my eyes becoming heavy, and before I know it I hear a deep voice beside me, and I sit up straight in my chair, realizing that I've been asleep.

"Miss," a man is saying.

I look up to see a policeman standing there, looking down at me. "Yes?"

"I wonder if I can ask you a few questions about the man you brought in this evening," he says, his voice kind.

I rub my eyes and sigh. "Sure."

He scribbles in a notebook as I tell him enough about Willie and myself to be helpful, without going into much detail. I explain that I only met him today, and that he lives on the streets, but that I feel like he's my friend.

"Whenever there's an obvious case of assault, the hospital calls us," he says. "We're just here to ask questions, is all."

"I understand," I say. Then I look at him. "When I was riding in the taxi, before I found Willie, I saw a group of young men—rather rough looking, I thought at the time—walking down Gull Street, I think. They were heading in the opposite direction."

The policeman raises his eyebrows and writes that down in his little book. "Can you describe them?"

All I can remember is that there were four or five of them dressed in bell bottom jeans, with long, greasy hair, one of them thin and one of them big and stout. A couple of them wore black jackets. "I'm afraid that's the best I can do," I tell him. "It was dark."

He snaps his notebook shut and shoves his pen into his pocket. "Well, thanks for your cooperation." He smiles at me.

Then a nurse is beside him, looking down at me. "Miss Muir?"

"Yes?"

The nurse looks over at the policeman. "Are you through, officer? I need to talk to her."

He nods. "I believe that's all I need for now. Good luck with your friend," he says to me, and walks away.

The nurse sits in the chair next to me. I'm afraid to hear what she might say. "Miss Muir—"

"Sera, please."

"Sera. What a pretty name."

"Is he alive?" I hear myself saying.

She nods. "For now. They're doing everything they can as we speak, but he's in critical condition. They've had to release pressure on his brain because of the swelling, and he has multiple fractures and contusions. I'm afraid he may not live through the night. I'm sorry."

I'm shocked Willie is still alive. "Is he in any pain?"

She shakes her head. "Nobody can answer that for sure. He's in a coma."

"Isn't there anything I can do?"

"He needs blood, and a lot of it. Do you know your blood type?"

"O positive, I think."

"We could use it, then."

I nod quickly. "Let's go," I say, jumping up, eager to help in any way I can.

After a nurse takes my blood and tapes a small bandage on my arm where the needle was, I ask if I can see Willie, but I'm told I have to go back and sit in the lobby and wait. When I get there the couple is gone but there are a few new people sitting and waiting, instead.

Finally a doctor comes out, his eyes tired. "Sera Muir?" he calls. I stand up.

"The nurse filled you in earlier about Willie," he says. "I'm afraid there's nothing further we can do now but wait. You might want to go on home and get some rest."

I blink. Home? I am as homeless as Willie. "I want to see him before I go," I say.

"I'm sorry, they only let immediate family up there."

"Then tonight he's my father," I tell him.

He stands there looking at me for a minute. Then he sighs and his mouth pulls into the hint of a smile—something that looks totally foreign on his otherwise stern features. "Come with me, then," he says.

Sunday, May 6, 1973

2:37 a.m.

Willie is so wrapped in bandages that it's hard to recognize that the thing on the bed is a person. There are tubes snaking out from everywhere, going up into his nose and his throat. Machines stand nearby, blipping and beeping and whooshing, and I suppose they are helping to keep him alive somehow. As active as the machines are, that is how still Willie lies there—still as death. The nurse tells me I can pull up a chair and sit at his side for awhile, and that's what I do. The nurse steps out, and it's just Willie and me.

I think about his energy signature—his life force—and wonder if it still resides in this body, and where it will go next. I wonder if there's something I could have done to keep this from happening to him. Could I have stayed longer this afternoon? Should I have gone ahead and given him the money instead of saving it in case I needed it? What if I hadn't shown up at all today—would it have changed things somehow? Would Willie be okay now instead of lying here broken and in a coma? I can't help feeling responsible for all the things gone wrong, although I cannot know if I am.

There must be something I can do for him. I dig for my first aid kit in the bag around my waist, and take out the remaining bandage. I unfold it and hold it up to him. The bandage is only an inch square, and looks ridiculous next to Willie's extensive injuries. It's only meant for shallow cuts. I stuff it back into the bag.

"You in there, Willie?" I whisper, leaning close. "It's me, Sera." I put a hand gently on one of his. "They'd know what to do for you at home," I tell him. "They could make you well."

There is no movement save the rise and fall of his chest to the rhythm of one of the machines. I get up and go to a window and look out. The hospital lights push against the fog outside, but just beyond, it is still night. Again I look in my little bag and pull something out. I sit down beside Willie and put it into his hand and close his fingers around it. "You believed in the magic of your shells," I say to him, and then I lay my head down on the bed next to him.

"Please make him whole again, God," I say. And I fall into a deep sleep, void of dreams until I find myself in the cold water, the sunlight glinting off the slap-slapping waves—but before the nightmare can continue . . .

Sunday, May 6, 1973

8:30 a.m.

... I'm awakened by the soft touch of the morning nurse, and I lift my head slowly, my neck stiff and sore from lying in one position. I look at Willie, lying still as before, with the machines beeping and whooshing around him.

The nurse checks them and smiles at me. "There's coffee downstairs."

"How is he?" I nod at Willie.

"No change, but he's still with us. The doctor will be in soon."

I rub my eyes, and look at my watch. *Eight-thirty—less than two hours left to find Lissa before my twenty-four hours is up.*

My stomach growls but I ignore it. The nurse has left the room. I look at Willie one last time, an ache in my heart.

I leave a wad of money with the lady at the desk—a different lady than the one last night. She looks at it and her eyebrows rise in surprise. We don't use money in my time, but I don't understand why everyone here looks at it as though they've never seen any of it before. It's just another mystery to me.

When I exit through the hospital's double doors, the brightness makes me blink. The sky is a clear, lovely blue, and a warm, gentle breeze plays in the small trees lining the main entrance, little birds singing on their leafy boughs. For a while last night, I had begun to think the sun would never come out again, that it would be dark forever.

Now I realize that I have no idea how to get back to the trailer. I had been in shock during our ride to the hospital, and now I'm totally lost. *I've got to find Lissa. I'm not going to make it in time.*

I turn to go back inside to see if I can call a taxi. Then I hear two short beeps of a horn. *Curtis.* I watch unbelieving as his taxi pulls right up alongside me in the circular drive. He grins and gets out, looking at me over the top of the car. "Hey, little lady," he says. "Where to?"

I can't help but laugh, relieved. "Don't tell me you've been waiting all night?"

"Naw, but I figured you'd still be here, maybe need a ride this morning. Thought it wouldn't hurt to check. Lucky timing, that's all. Need a ride?"

"*Do* I."

When I get in I can see that Curtis has spread a seat cover over the back to hide the stains, and I'm grateful I can't see them.

"Where are we going?" he asks.

"Back to the trailer. But just let me off on the main road. I'll walk to it."

"Sure thing."

"You're a lifesaver, Curtis," I tell him as we start off.

He looks at me in the mirror. "How's the old man?"

I don't tell him that Willie is probably younger than him—that his way of life has made him ancient before his time. I look out at the passing scenery. "Not good. They did the best they could, but he's in a coma. They don't expect him to live much longer."

"Tough break," he says. "I don't know why anybody'd want to mess with an old man like that. Don't make any sense. Hope they catch the bastards who did it—pardon my French."

"Me too."

In stark contrast to the stillness of the night before, people are out in throngs this morning. The roads are busy, the parking lots packed, the sidewalks full of families and shoppers and tourists, no doubt typical to a coastal town. Except for all the children, this is more like what I'm used to, if on a much smaller scale. Although I never thought I'd miss the confusion, I find it somehow comforting. At least it's something I understand.

I think about Gabe and I touch my face where his warm hands were cupped gently around it. Now that moment seems surreal and far away. I haven't called him and he probably thinks I'm angry with him. But there's nothing I can do about that. Maybe in some way it's for the best.

When we arrive at the trailer park, I hand Curtis one of the hundred-dollar bills. "I insist you take this and get yourself a new backseat or something. I'm not getting out of this car until you take it."

He looks at me and I stare at him defiantly, folding my arms across my chest. Finally he shakes his head and laughs. "You're somethin' else, young lady. You know that?" He tips his cap to me when I get out. "Good luck to you."

I wave at him as he drives off. "I'm going to need it," I say out loud, walking down the sandy main driveway to the trailer park.

As I approach the old beige trailer, I'm disappointed to see the bus is still not parked in the drive. In the back of my tired mind I had been hoping that Lissa somehow had made it back to the Beauty Barn and driven home, but now that I'm focused on her again, it would make more sense, if she was really on the run, to walk home instead. The only alternative for her would be to hitch a ride with someone and maybe leave town altogether. I shudder to think of it, and stop beside the trailer, wondering what to do next.

I can hear voices inside, just like yesterday, the first time I came here. I hear Gabe's low voice, and another, higher one. *Lissa?* I move quietly around to the other side of the trailer where the ramp is, and am surprised to see a strange car parked on this side, up close to the door. Someone else is here. Now I hear another voice, an even higher one, but it isn't the voice of a child. It's another woman—a friend, perhaps? I move closer to the side of the trailer and listen. A window is open and I can make out part of an intense conversation.

"You have to go turn yourself in, then, and explain everything to them. *You don't have any choice, Lissa,*" Gabe is saying.

"I ain't going to jail, Gabe. And that's where I'll be if I turn myself in, and you know it. You hate me because of—because of what I done. But I'm still the mother of your children. You want them to hang me or something? Is that what you want?"

Then another woman's voice—high and nasal: "Don't be stupid, Lissa. They don't hang nobody anymore. They use the electric chair or—"

"*Stop it,* Cindy," Gabe says, angry. "You can't run forever, Lissa. Where would you go? That wouldn't be any kind of life—and I wouldn't let you take the kids, so just put that right out of your head. Now, you said the man was alive when you left him."

"I swear it. You believe me, don't you Gabe? *Gabe?*" Lissa says tearfully.

Now it's quiet, and I can imagine Gabe sitting in his chair, the shock of learning his wife truly was with another man still fresh.

"You may do a lot of things, but it isn't in you to murder someone. I believe you," he says. "And they will, too."

I hear Lissa crying. "They ain't gonna believe somebody like me. Brian's father has them expensive lawyers. They'll get me all mixed up and I'll say something stupid. We got no money for a decent lawyer—we ain't got shit. You're supposed to *protect me*, Gabe. *I don't want to go to prison.*"

All I can hear for a minute is the sound of Lissa sobbing. I wonder where Hailey and Bug are, and hope they're not able to hear all this.

All of a sudden Cindy's high voice rings out. "It's the cops—oh Lissa, they're coming for you!"

I move quickly and peek around the side of the trailer. A police car is coming slowly down the sandy road, its tires churning up dust. I look around wildly for someplace to hide, but see nothing—not even a shrub. Then I remember the car parked next to the ramp. I crawl into the backseat and hunch down.

The back door of the trailer bursts open. Lissa runs down the ramp, fumbling with a set of keys. She jumps into the front seat of the car and starts it up.

Cindy scrambles down the ramp after her. "Wait, Lissa—wait for me. *Hey!* Dammit, it's my car—you can't just take it! *Come back.*"

Gabe appears in the door, his face white. "Lissa, don't leave like this," he yells.

But she isn't listening to anyone. She drives over the sparse grass behind the trailers so she can't be seen, down to where she can get beyond the police car and onto the sandy road that leads to the highway.

8

Lissa

If anybody had told me that one day I'd be running from the cops because of a murder rap, I'd have laughed in their face and called them a fool. And if anybody had told me I was gonna watch somebody kicked to death in front of my eyes that same night, I'd have told them they were a *crazy ass* fool. Nothing like that ever happens around here, much less to me. Sure, I used to fantasize about torturing those boys who used to tease me so bad in school, but it ain't like I would ever really have done anything.

I feel so alone it hurts, more than I ever thought possible. Thing is, before, I *always* knew what to do in a mess—but not anymore. The only thing I know now is, I have to pull myself together and make a plan.

I crouch down on the beach behind some dunes for a while, shivering in the dark because I'm cold and afraid. Somehow, in spite of it all, I fall asleep, and the next thing I know, I'm opening my eyes to a pink sky where the sun is rising. I don't even get the luxury of thinking the whole ugly thing might just have been a nightmare when I first wake up, either, 'cause I'm lying out here on the frigging beach. I sit up and wipe the sand off where it's stuck to me. I'm shivering real good now.

I stay where I am for a while to get my bearings, and finally I decide the best thing for me to do is to follow the beach on down until I get to where the trailer park is. My stomach takes a turn when I think about going home and facing Gabe and the kids, but mostly Gabe. If I go home I'm gonna have to tell him what happened, 'cause he's going to find out anyway. I don't know what it is I want from him, but without the bus or my money, it's the only thing to do until I can figure a way to get out of here altogether. Besides, I'm tired and cold and hungry, and I got no other place to go.

It takes me a long time to walk down the beach that far, 'cause every time I see somebody walking toward me I have to duck behind a dune or stoop over and pretend I'm looking at shells or something, but I finally get to the little boardwalk with the bench on it that comes down from the trailer park, and I head up the path to our trailer.

I stop in my tracks. There's a car parked beside the trailer. I'm about to turn around and run back where I came from, till I see it's Cindy's car. "*Shit*," I say, staring at it. She's either so nosy she had to come see for herself what trouble I'm in, or she came 'cause Gabe called her, asking where I am. Either way, it ain't gonna be good.

The sun is getting higher over the water, and I decide I can't wait any longer; I just got to go in. So I climb the ramp and go inside.

Gabe sees me first and comes into the kitchen, his eyes all big. "My God, Lissa—where have you been?"

Cindy turns around to look at me. She's standing behind him and shakes her head at me like she hasn't told him anything yet.

"Where's the kids?" I ask him.

"Auntie Ada has them," Cindy says. "Gabe asked if she could watch them while we looked for you. I just got back from driving them over. She even skipped going to church this morning." She laughs—a fake, hollow one.

I take a deep breath. "There's something I got to tell you, Gabe. Don't say a word till I get through." I collapse on the sofa and put my head in my hands and tell him everything. Cindy sets there with her mouth open like she can't believe I'm really telling him, Gabe with his jaw all set and his face getting pale. When I'm through, he looks at me and then at Cindy. She looks away so she doesn't have to look at his eyes.

The silence is so long it makes me sick. "Say something, Gabe," I tell him.

I feel his eyes on me. When he speaks his voice is choked up but calm. "Why didn't you tell me last night?" he asks. "Why didn't you just come home so we could figure out what to do?"

"I don't know. I was scared. I wanted to find my ring. Maybe I thought everything would be okay if I could just find my ring." My voice tapers off to a whisper and my eyes sting with fresh tears. Cindy's staring at the floor and fiddling with her keys.

Gabe is talking to me, and I have to look up and say, "What?"

"I said, you have to go to the police and explain everything to them. *You don't have any choice, Lissa.*"

We argue for awhile, 'cause I ain't about to turn myself in. I'm looking at him while he's talking to me and I realize he ain't gonna help me after all, and I'm really on my own. I really start bawling, 'cause everything's caving in on me and I can't see any way out.

Cindy's standing at the front window; she starts going crazy, pointing outside and telling me the cops are coming for me. I can't even think and don't want to anymore. I just jump up and grab the keys out of her hand and run out the kitchen door—something I should have done when I first got here instead of going through all this shit. Gabe and Cindy are yelling at me as I get in her car.

I drive it through all the pitiful little sandy yards till I get clear of the cops, and floor it when I'm out on the highway.

I gotta tell you, with these wheels moving fast under me, I feel freer than I have for what seems days now—but it's only been hours. The houses and land fly by me in a blur. The first thing I'll do, I think, is head right out of town, and drive till I can't drive another mile, and see where it gets me. I don't bother to even think about what I'll do for money or gas, 'cause the tank is nearly full and I know the cops are back there and they'll try to catch up to me soon. But by then I plan to be out of the county, at least. Then I'll worry about what to do next. Something will come up—it always does, doesn't it?

I drive along, forcing myself to maintain the speed limit so I won't look suspicious in case there's a cop over the next hill. Then I get a glimpse of something in the rearview mirror. *There's somebody in here with me.*

I stifle a scream, and yell instead, "*Who the hell's back there?*"

Slowly somebody's head comes up from the backseat. I'm fighting back hysteria. "You? The babysitter? Why the hell are you in my car?"

She leans back as if she's scared of me. "It's Sera, Lissa. Don't be scared."

"Scared? Of you?" I laugh, and it sounds like a woman gone crazy. "What the hell do you think you're doing?" I steer the car around a corner and the tires screech loudly.

"Please slow down," she says. "I need to talk to you. That's all. I want to help you. I know what's happening to you. I know everything."

I look at her in the mirror too long, and the tires go off the side of the road into the soft, sandy shoulder. I have to think quick to get us back on the road without wrecking. "Look," I tell her, "if you're so almighty smart and you know what's happening, then you know I gotta get out of here *now*—I don't have time for a nice little chit-chat. I'm gonna stop up here, and then you just get out and go back to wherever you came from."

I wait till I see a turnoff, then pull over into the gravel. "Now get out," I yell at her.

She's setting there, eyes all big, looking about as ragged as me—her hair all sticking out, face smudged with dust. And I see what looks like blood on her dress. "The hell happened to you?"

She looks down and back up at me, her face scrunched up like she could cry. "My friend was in an accident. I didn't have time to change. Look—" She leans forward. "I can't explain it, Lissa; there isn't much time. You have to trust me. Something bad is going to happen very soon unless you do." She looks at her watch and back at me. "It's almost time. You can't run anymore right now. We have to stay right here, in this car, so you'll be safe. And get away from the water."

I stare at her and throw up my hands. "What are you, some kind of freakin' sideshow crystal ball seer or something? Ain't it enough, what I've been through the last twenty-four hours, without *you*?" I'm yelling, and my voice is hoarse.

She looks scared, like she thinks I'm off my rocker, and I gotta admit I might be by now. I try to calm down so she'll just get out and leave me alone. "Look," I say. "I don't know what you're talking about, but the longer I stay here, the more trouble I'm gonna be in. So if you really give a shit about whether or not I'm safe, get the hell out of my car. That's all I gotta say."

She just folds her arms and leans back. "Okay, you asked for it. I'm *you*, Lissa. I'm you in the future, and I've come back to keep you from dying today. Think about it. How else would I know to be here right now?"

I shake my head, unable to think of what to say to this crazy fool.

"I know all about you," she says. "Ask me anything."

"I don't have time—"

"*Ask* me."

"What's my mother's name?"

"Andrea."

"Where did I go to school?"

"Bridgeland Elementary, Stillwell Junior High, Oak Island High School. Oh—and a few months at Peachville Beauty College, until you ran out of money."

"Lucky guess. What's my favorite color?"

That seems to shut her up for a second. "Green," she says. "The color of money."

I look at her then. Even though she's right, I still think she's nuts—and she's determined to stay in the car. I'm going to have to get back on the road with her flapping her jaws at me whether I like it or not. "I'm getting out of here," I tell her. "You wanna stay back there, it's up to you, but I'm not sitting here waiting for cops. Last chance."

She shakes her head. "I'm staying."

I turn the key and start the engine. A car whooshes by and turns into the gravel in front of us. My heart races and I think it's all over, till I see who it is getting out. As she walks around her car to my side, I see Sera duck down in the back again. I start to tell her there ain't any need, that this is a friend, but right then Becka sticks her frizzy head in the window. I turn the car off again.

"*Becka?*" I say. "What are you doing here?"

She stands back from the car a little, and I can see she's dressed in her white hospital uniform. "Cindy was kind enough to call me this morning and tell me what was going on. Why didn't *you* tell me, Lissa? Aren't we friends anymore?"

I shake my head. "I figured you wouldn't want to be involved, I guess. I didn't do nothing, you know. The other night, I mean. But the cops think I did. It's nice of you to find me and all, but I gotta get out of here. Don't worry about me."

She squints in the bright sun. "But I do worry about you, Lissa. I worry about you a lot. I always have."

"I gotta go, Becka. Please just move out of the way."

But she stands there looking at me. "I worried about you when we were in junior high and high school together, and you always seemed to get the guy."

I look at her, not understanding. "What are you talking about?"

"Pretty Lissa, the guys always drooling over you. Didn't you know?"

I shake my head, my face getting hot.

"Every time I was interested in a boy, you got to him first. Every time."

"That isn't true, Becka. You went out with lots of guys—"

"I went out with *losers*, because you took all the good ones. There was quite a string of them—but let's take Gabe, for instance. The most important one of all. When I first saw him, I wanted him more than anyone else in the whole world. When he took Cindy out, I wasn't worried. I knew it wouldn't last and it didn't. When they split up, did you know Gabe was just getting around to asking me out? It's true. We talked in the hall one day for a long time, and he was real nice to me. I could tell he liked me, Lissa. And it was only a matter of time and he would have asked me. But you stepped in and got your claws into him. I never had a chance after that. It wasn't fair."

I stare at her, and there's hate in her eyes. Her hands are pulled into fists at her sides.

"I didn't know, Becka." I say. "You never *said* you were interested in him."

She laughs and pounds a fist on top of the car. "Real friends are supposed to know things like that. You didn't care about me enough to ask, did you—you just assumed that someone as popular as Gabe could never be interested in me. It never even crossed your mind, did it?" She clenches her teeth. "It just made me so mad!"

I open my mouth to say something, but she stomps a foot.

"*Shut up*," she says. "Always talking, always talking. Can't you just *shut up?*" She moves close to my window and I shrink back in the seat.

"I wanted you to pay for that, Lissa. I wanted to see to it you never got what you wanted, that Gabe wouldn't be able to be a big basketball star after all, and you wouldn't get your big, fancy house and your fancy red convertible—I wanted to see you suffer."

Her eyes narrow in her white face, her hair blowing around it like flames. "Who do you think was in the other car that dark, rainy night Gabe and his friends ended up in a ditch? Oh yes—there were two cars coming from opposite directions on the slick road, one of them swerving at the last second to hit the other one head-on. Unfortunately for them, the people in one of those cars weren't familiar with that one little rule about how to stay in the game—the most important rule of all. Which meant at the last second they swerved to avoid the other car and ended up in that big ditch. It's almost funny, you know? Those guys may have shot a mean game of basketball, but they were just plain lousy at playing chicken. I guess no one can be good at everything.

"Now I want you to think, Lissa. Think real hard. Who could that brave person have been in that other car that night? Who could possibly be cool enough to keep the steering wheel trained straight and true so the car was headed right for that other set of headlights no matter what? Surely it couldn't have been sweet, little old wallflower Becka, could it?"

My mouth drops open and I put a hand on my heart to keep it from beating out of my chest. "Becka—*no*. You're lying."

She laughs. "I didn't figure on Gabe surviving, but it turned out to be a bonus. Because all these years I've gotten to watch you struggling through the days, tired and bitter, working at some menial job to make money to support two kids and a crippled husband that'll never amount to anything—while I do whatever I please and have a job that really *means* something. You want to know something *really* funny? Turns out you got the loser, not me."

I sit up straight in my seat. "Get out of my way, Becka," I tell her, fumbling with the key in the ignition.

She backs up but she's still talking. "And what about Brian, Lissa?"

I stop and look at her. "What about him?"

"You didn't learn your lesson, did you?" she says. "You just go on and on and you don't learn."

"*What about Brian?*" I yell, ready to leap out of the car and strangle Becka.

She rolls her eyes. "I wanted Brian. I saw him up at the bar *first*, even before Cindy, and I was going to go over to him later on, after you and Cindy left. He was lonely, Lissa. I had it all planned out, what I was going to say to him and everything. I really had a chance. After all, I knew Cindy wouldn't go for him—rich, popular guys have always intimidated her when it comes right down to it. She said herself he was out of our league. And you? You're *supposed* to be a married woman, remember? I know you flirt around and all, but I thought you would at least honor your marriage vows. But *no*—you had to get him in your sights. I knew that look in your eyes only too well, and that it was only a matter of time. So I made Cindy take me home, and then I got in my car and came back and waited. You didn't see me because I was around the other side in the shadows, but I was there. I got out of my car and walked right up to the bus and watched the whole thing through the window, Lissa, and neither one of you even knew. It was disgusting.

"I couldn't just let you get away with it—messing up my plans again. I wasn't sure what I was going to do, but it turned out all I had to do was wait, because you just left him there in the gravel—as loyal and caring as always. Then all I had to do was kill him. It wasn't hard—he was so out of it he barely even struggled when I put the rag down his throat and he suffocated."

Now I'm crying. I can't believe Becka is saying these things. I put my hands over my ears—I just want her to stop. But she doesn't.

"Oh, I had to make sure the police would find a certain little trinket so they'd know where to look for the *real* culprit. Your wedding ring." She wags her index finger at me and *tsk*s. "You must have dropped it in the parking lot. I made sure to put it next to Brian. The idiot police didn't find it at first, so I had to drop it in an envelope and put it in the mail with a little typewritten note. I'm sure they'll be very interested in what it has to say."

"Bitch," I say under my breath. I start up the car and floor it, gravel flying up at Becka and onto her car. I swerve around it and onto the road, almost losing control for a long moment. Sera's head shoots up from the backseat and when I glance in the mirror she looks as terrified as me. For a second I get the eerie feeling that I'm looking in a mirror at myself.

"My God, she's the one," Sera says.

"What?"

"She's the one that's going to try to kill you, Lissa. Don't you believe me now?"

I suck in ragged breaths and my voice comes out hoarse. "All I know is, I'm getting out of here. You better hold on."

9

Sera

Sunday, May 6, 1973

10:07 a.m.

I glance at my watch, and Mickey's hands tell me our time is almost up. I feel as though I'm on a runaway train, and there's nothing I can do to stop it. I hold my breath and clutch the sides of the seat as Lissa drives fast over the high bridge that spans the waterway. I let out my breath with sheer relief. At least now the water is behind us. Lissa is determined to get away—*or is she?*

She turns the wheel hard and the tires scream as the tail end of the car reels around in the road until we're facing the way we came. And then we head back over the bridge. On the other side, she turns hard onto a narrow road that leads away from the waterway, but meets and then runs alongside a branch of the Cape Fear River. She's no longer on the highway, but heading back toward town. I can see how the road we're on winds around close to the edge of the river, which at this point rushes along about fifty feet downhill from us.

"Where are you going?" I yell at the back of her head, her hair flying in my face.

"I gotta go back and tell them what she done," Lissa yells back.

"But the water—get away from the water," I tell her. "She's going to try to drown you. *Listen to me*—"

A car pulls up, racing alongside us, forcing us into the left lane closest to the water. Lissa and I turn to see Becka leaning out her window and hollering, her eyes wild. She doesn't appear to see me in the backseat at all, perhaps because of the sun's glare—or perhaps she's just blind with anger.

Lissa turns her attention to driving, trying to speed ahead, but the road is narrow and she has to focus on staying on it. I can hear Becka yelling at the top of her voice to be heard above the wind: "I'm gonna stop you for good this time, Lissa. I'm gonna make real good and sure you get what you deserve."

Becka slams the side of her car into ours. There's a sharp jolt, and Lissa's fighting the wheel to the right, trying to keep the car on the road. The left side of the car screeches against the guardrail, sending cold chills to my very bones.

"My God, Lissa—get us away from the water," I hear myself yell, my heart pounding in my throat.

"I'm trying," she screams back. "She's got us hemmed in."

Becka falls back on a long curve. Lissa floors it coming out of the bend.

"I'm losing her," Lissa yells.

I turn around. Becka is coming up fast.

"She's catching up, Lissa—hurry."

We veer around another long bend, the road now in a sharp decline, carrying us closer to the water below. I turn; somehow Becka is next to us again, grinning, her red hair flying all around. I watch her wink at Lissa, and then her lips mouth the word *Gotcha*. She turns the wheel and rams us again.

This time Lissa loses control. The car crunches as it scrapes the guardrail, and then it breaks through. We sail into the air, hurtling over jagged rocks—falling, falling, falling, until we hit the water below in one loud, smashing, watery blow that sends us both into the seats, into the ceiling.

My thigh bangs hard against the door handle. I think I black out for a second; when I come to, there's water gushing in the open window beside me. I'm dizzy; my head hurts. Even so, I crawl through the window into the cold, salty water of the river.

I start sinking, and thrash at the rushing water. Somehow I manage to keep my head above it. A rock juts from the river nearby; I grab onto it, my breath ragged. The car gurgles loudly as it sinks, as the air escapes from inside it. My heart leaps as I think of Lissa, and I look around wildly to see if she might have gotten out—no sign of her.

From my vantage point behind the rock, I can see Becka up the hill, peering over the broken guardrail, her hand at her forehead to shield her eyes from the bright sun on the water. Again, I feel she can't see me, and I know she's surveying her handiwork. When she turns and disappears, I look for Lissa again. I fear she's trapped in the car, which is now almost totally underwater.

"Lissa!" I yell. No answer. I look at the water roiling all around me and taste blood in my mouth.

I move around the rock to where I can see down into the car. Lissa is pressed against the driver's side, blood on her face. Her eyes are wide open in terror, and she's holding her breath now, looking up at me through the murky, cold water.

"Lissa," I yell again, "get out!"

But she's shaking her head and reaching up for me through the window, as though she's trapped inside the crumpled car and can't move.

Everything seems to move in slow motion now as my nightmare unfolds before my very eyes. Only I'm not the one sinking in the murk, it's Lissa. I'm not looking up at someone for help—it's she looking up at me. *I'm* the white face with the two dark places for eyes that looks down at her. And I know what she's feeling—that her lungs are burning and she doesn't understand why I won't help her—

But that *is* me—Sera—long ago. My dream has been a memory all along, as Dr. Moore said it might be. And now I'm watching it happen all over again. I'm watching myself drown.

All of this and more runs through my mind in a second. I see my mother's picture, her beautiful smile and the tilt of her head. I see my father looking at me from behind his huge desk, disappointment in his eyes. I see Thomas laughing and holding up chopsticks, noodles dangling from them. I see Willie—his dark face animated as he talks to me, then the same face swathed in bandages as he lies near death. I see Gabe's face, close to mine as we touch lips.

All this in one second, and I'm back in the cold, swirling water, looking down at Lissa's face, seeing her lips growing blue and her eyes glazing over. I can see myself in those eyes—the fear, the realization, the hopelessness. But knowing that we are the same entity doesn't matter anymore—she's just a young woman who desperately wants to live. And now I understand why I'm really here.

To save us both.

I let go of the rock and slide down into the water until I grab onto Lissa's outstretched hand. I pull as hard as I can, but she is lodged within.

Come on, you can make it, Lissa, I think, willing her to hear me. *You're not alone anymore—I won't let go of you.*

Now there is too much water, too much darkness, and we're both being pulled down with the car, sinking as the hard, metallic bulk of it sucks us down into the dark, cold gloom. Still I grasp Lissa's hand, her grip now too weak to hold mine. But I don't let go.

I don't let go.

10

Willie

Thursday, May 20, 2202

2:29 p.m.

I thought I'd died and passed on to the Other Side. One minute I'm lying in a gray fog, the next there's a beam of light reaching out to take me through a dark tunnel, just like I read about in a magazine one time. Then I'm lying in Heaven, 'cause it's bright and soft and quiet, with two of the Lord's holy angels dressed in white looking down at me—one beautiful angel, and one ugly, bald one. And they look to be about as surprised to see me as I am to see them.

I open my mouth to greet them, but a pain washes over me and I wonder how it can be so bad, 'cause it's Heaven, don't you know. Then I fall back into that gray fog again.

Some time later, when I wake up, I learn I'm not in Heaven at all. Turns out them holy angels are doctors—Dr. Moore and Dr. Weiss—which calls to mind something Sera told me. They're the ones, sent her on her great journey through time. They tell me I've been asleep for two weeks now, and that I'm almost ready.

"For what?" I ask.

"To be dismissed from the hospital," the bald one tells me.

I look around me. It's strange—I ain't in no hospital bed; I'm sitting up in a chair by the window. I look down at myself, expecting to see bandages, but there ain't a one—all the cuts and bruises are gone like they were never even there. I put my hands to my face and it feels about right, 'cept there's something bothering me about my mouth I can't quite put a finger on.

Dr. Moore smiles at me and holds out a mirror, so I take it and hold it up to myself. I can't believe my own eyes. It looks like me, but it don't. The last time I looked at myself in a mirror was at the old gas station, one time when somebody left the door unlocked. When I looked at my face, it was like an old man looking back at me. But now the face in the mirror is so fresh looking I can't help but break out in a big smile, and when I do, I got all my teeth in my head again, like when I was young.

At first I'm so surprised I can't say nothing, but then I say, "This is like being born into a brand new world, only without the spanking. How did you do that?" I ask them, still staring at my teeth.

"I don't know," Dr. Weiss says. "That's someone else's field of expertise. I'm just a lowly scientist." He breaks into a smile.

They tell me I was almost dead when they got me.

"But how did I get here?" I ask them. "I remember Sera told me folks from the past couldn't be brought up here to the future."

Dr. Weiss looks at Dr. Moore, who touches my shoulder. "It was supposed to be impossible," she admits. "When Sera didn't communicate with us at the critical time, we made the decision to lock on her energy signature and go ahead with retrieval. But you showed up instead. We were rather shocked, until our medical doctors did a thorough workup on you, and discovered that your veins contain some of Sera's blood, still fresh in your body, which could only mean that she gave it to help your doctors back there. Our EyeCom locked onto it instead of Sera, and brought you back."

Dr. Weiss, beside her, nods. "If I hadn't seen it with my own eyes, I wouldn't have thought it possible."

I sit up and put down the mirror. "Then what about Sera? When will she get back home?"

This time Dr. Moore drops her eyes and looks away. Dr. Weiss looks at me. "She can't come home, Willie," he says, his voice soft. "We've lost her."

"What do you mean, you lost her?" I look from one to the other. "What about that EyeCom thing you got?"

"There's been a terrible accident," Dr. Weiss says. "There was an anomaly that even fooled EyeCom. We originally mistook the drowning to be that of her past entity, when in reality it was her own. Her energy signature unique to our present time is no longer valid. It has been assimilated into the past. There simply isn't anything of the woman we knew as Sera for EyeCom to lock onto anymore."

I look at him, not understanding.

"I'm afraid Sera is dead," he says. "We can never bring her home."

I don't want to believe that sweet little Sera is dead. I look straight at Dr. Weiss. "Did I do this?" I ask him outright. "Did it happen because somehow I came back instead of her?"

Dr. Moore speaks up. "No, Willie. If Sera had been alive, EyeCom would have picked up on her signature right away. It was searching for her when it finally found the remnants of her in you. She was already gone. We aren't sure what happened, except she was with her past entity when she died."

"Lissa," I say.

She looks surprised. "Yes. How did you know?"

"Sera and I got to be friends. She bought me a cheeseburger. It was a real good one, too." My heart feels heavy and my eyes water. "I liked that young lady. I can't believe she's gone."

Dr. Moore turns her head to the wall. "I am most responsible for her death. I persuaded her to go, told her it was safe, for God's sake. She trusted me."

I don't know what to say to this Dr. Moore. Sometimes it's best not to say a thing and just let it be.

We're all three of us quiet for a time.

"How'd you know my name is Willie?" I ask Dr. Moore.

"Sera told us about you. I've known her a long time, Willie. I could tell she liked you, that you made a big impression on her."

Now is when I got to cry for a little while.

* * *

Well, Dr. Moore and Dr. Weiss taught me everything I need to know, now I'm here, 'cause they say it's impossible for me to go back—things wouldn't work out right, since I'm special. And although it hurts them to do it, they abandon their time travel until more of the bugs can be worked out—maybe in a few years, maybe never. They don't want any more accidents.

I think on that awhile, and decide that if things really do end up working out the way the good Lord wants them to, maybe I'm meant to be here. I only wish Sera and Goblin could be here with me; it doesn't seem right that they aren't. Even way up here in the future, there's things I'll never understand.

They say my body is cured and so is my mind, but aside from that stranger, looks at me in the mirror, I ain't seen much difference yet—although I admit I ain't seen anything so far, looks like an alien, and that feels mighty good.

Some lawyers come to the hospital the day I was leaving and told me I'm heir to Sera's fortune. I told them I don't know anything about that, and they must have the wrong man, but they said, "Well, you're Willie, aren't you?" and when I said, "I am," they patted me on the back and winked at me and said, "Then you're the only *blood* relative she has."

Dr. Moore smiled at me and said, "Sera would have liked that, Willie. That would have been just like her."

I told them I don't reckon I can argue with that, so they took me to her apartment home, way up in a building so high I can see the birds flying below me when I look out the glass doors, and they give me the keys.

The kind of man's lived in a cardboard box ain't the kind of man comfortable with all I got now. But I remember a day long ago when I found a twenty in the parking lot of Piggly Wiggly, and I think the Lord must be entrusting me with Sera's money, so I aim to do something with it that might help people and make her proud. To do my best, I'm gonna have to think on it for a time. I got myself some ideas knocking around in my head, though. Maybe I'll build a ball field for the kids to play in. I understand they ain't many of them left, so maybe they need a place to get up a game on Saturday afternoons, see what it really feels like to just be a kid. Maybe I'll find out if there's folks that could use a place to get on their feet when they down and out, like I was for so long.

Also there's that big house Sera's father lived in, which I'm gonna sell, since it reminded her of bad times. I went there just to see it, and nearly died from fright when a funny looking metal man like from the Wizard of Oz came up, asking me if he could get me something. I *start* to tell him he can get me a dry pair of pants.

Anyway, I think it's old Willie's place now to make things right for Sera, and tie up loose ends.

When I visit Sera's old boss Derek at the Cosmos Coffee Shop, I have to break it to him Sera ain't coming back. At first he's standing there shining up the countertop with a rag like it's the most important job in the world, but he stops when I tell him about her. He acts genuine sorry to hear it, too.

"She was a good person," he says. I tell him I know it.

He tells me sit down and he'll get me a cup of something if I want, and I tell him a plain old cup of coffee would be nice, if they's still such a thing as that. Then we talk for awhile. He says he's thinking about closing down 'cause he just ain't got the business anymore.

"I got a young wife wants a baby more than anything, but we're never going to get one at this rate. Today I only had five customers. People are tired of the same old thing," he says, pointing to the menu on the wall. "I can't say as I blame them."

Then I get me an idea. "How 'bout you and me getting together an' opening a *real* restaurant?" I say to him. "One that's got real home-cooked food in it."

"I don't know anything about cooking, Willie," he tells me.

"*I do*, and I know what folks are hungry for," I say. "There's some things, don't change much through the years. I'll do the cooking; you do the cleaning up."

"But who would we get to take orders?" he says. "Nobody seems to want to work."

"I got a certain robot in mind—he's just aching to get somebody something. He's in need of a good job."

He stands there looking at me for a minute, fumbling with the rag, and then his face lights up and he shakes my hand. "Ripping," he says, which I learned in futurespeak means he thinks that would be just fine.

* * *

The first night I saw the Wheel, I thought it was the second most beautiful thing I ever laid eyes on, Iris being the first. I watched it gliding through the city like it was floating on the air, and then, when it got closer, I saw it *was*. And the folks on it were lit up like little cities themselves, and full of a peculiar joy I ain't ever seen before in a human being. Makes me wonder why they're so full of raw joy like that, 'cause their world is still full of troubles like it's always been. They just got different ones piled on top of more of the same, seems to me.

Then I hear my papa's voice telling me, *Folks all just trying to live, son. We all just trying to find our way.* And I think maybe the bigger the troubles you got, the more you need to celebrate the little things, like just being alive, and that's what they're doing, even if they don't know it.

I planted a young oak tree in a field outside the city in Sera's name. It's little now, but someday it'll grow up big and strong, its branches reaching up to the sky. This morning I've brought some pretty wildflowers to set beside the tree, with its little oak leaves fluttering in the warm summer breeze.

I take her wooden token out of my pocket and hold it up. They say it was in my hand when I got here, and I was holding onto it so tight, they could barely pry it loose. I know she must have put it there, 'cause I recall her telling me about it. When I hold it to the sky like this and let the sun shine down on it, its carved star shape looks right at home up there in all that blue, and I think what an amazing little creature it is the Lord put on this earth, that can make itself whole again.

I like to think of Sera that way. I like to believe that when that bad accident happened to her and Lissa, somehow their two broken souls came together to make a whole, new, fresh one, and that a part of Sera still lives on back there.

Now, there's folks, might want to call old Willie crazy for thinking such a thing as that, even though them doctors say they got my brain fixed up right as rain. But if having faith is crazy, then I reckon that's what I am after all.

11

Lissa

Friday, June 17, 1973

3:45 p.m.

Early this afternoon, Gabe and Hailey and Bug and me bring a picnic lunch over to the boardwalk and eat it right there, with the sun shining down and the breeze grabbing our napkins so we have to keep running after them. Bug takes it upon himself to be responsible for Gabe's; the last time it blew away, he threw down his cookie and went out and fetched it before it could go too far. He proudly brought it back, all sandy and wet.

"I got Daddy's nakkin," he announced to me, and I winked at him.

When we first got here, I took the kids right out on the beach for a few minutes before lunch. All of a sudden I had a bad dizzy spell, looking out at all that water, which Gabe tells me is probably because of what happened in the accident. I can't remember anything about that. But anyway, the dizziness finally went away, and when it did the ocean seemed to take on a kind of beauty like I ain't ever seen—the different shades of blues and greens of the water dancing and playing on each other in the sunlight, the foamy surf unrolling itself on the white sand like a soft, magic carpet at our bare feet.

Looking at it like that makes me feel like a kid again, myself.

After we've finished eating everything in the basket, Gabe and I lean back and watch the kids go running in the sand with their kite, the wind lifting it into the air so easy that soon it ain't nothing but a little red diamond in the sky.

Gabe laughs, getting a big kick over how excited they are, and I look at him and think about everything that's happened in the last weeks.

I remember waking up in the hospital room for the first time after the accident, not really all there enough to even open my eyes, but I could hear voices somewhere in the room with me. I recognized Gabe and my mama talking, and I listened for a minute while I floated in some hazy place.

"But who was the young woman they found washed down the river, under the bridge?" Mama was asking.

Gabe spoke to her quiet and low. "Her name was Sera. We met her only the day before—she was interested in babysitting, and Lissa decided to see how it would work out. The kids really took to her while she was here. She offered to look for Lissa when she didn't come home, and she must have ended up getting tangled up in something along with Lissa. Nobody's sure, but she may have been in the car with Lissa when the accident happened, or maybe she was walking along that street and saw the car go over and tried to help. Anyway, her body was found where you heard—downriver, under the big bridge. The police asked me a lot of questions about her. They have no records of Sera even existing. They're wondering if she might even have caused the accident. But I don't believe it. In any case, we'll never know unless Lissa can tell us."

Mama said, "It's a blessing those fishermen happened on the scene when they did—my poor little girl clinging to that rock in the water, dazed and half drowned. I just don't understand what happened to make Lissa go off the road like that. Her father taught her to drive, you know, before he died. I remember watching the two of them from the front window, thinking how fast she'd grown up. I can see that picture in my mind now, like it was this morning. Ain't time such a funny thing, Gabe."

Then it was like a shade was pulled down over my mind, and everything faded away again.

Next time when I woke up, I could open my eyes. I saw I was in a hospital room, and the first thing I focused on was a clear plastic bag filled with some kind of goop, with a tube hanging from it taped to my arm. I looked at the stand next to the bed and the clock on it said nine thirty-five, and I figured by the little slice of sky I could see through the blinds that it had to be nighttime.

"Where is everybody?" I tried saying, but my throat was dry and raspy and it came out funny. So I pushed a little red button that I figured would get a nurse in there, although I think there must have been a shift change going on or something.

Before I could even lean back on my pillow, a girl in a white uniform walked in carrying a stack of towels. She dropped the whole stack on the floor with a *whump*, so I looked at her to see what happened, and she was looking at me with her eyes about popping out of her head. Then her mouth flew open and she screamed—a shrill, piercing sound that rang in my head like the old school bell used to do, so I put my hands up to my ears. I was scared—I didn't understand what *she* was so damned scared of.

Next there was footsteps coming loud down the hall, and what seemed like a crowd of people poured into the room—a couple of nurses followed by a doctor followed by Gabe and my mama, and even a cop. They stared at the girl too, but she didn't seem to know they were in the room with us. She was still staring at me and it freaked me out, so I drew the covers up to my chin.

Then the girl opened her mouth. "No, it isn't true. You're dead; I saw you. I saw the car take you under."

I didn't know what she was talking about. I just stared back at her white face and her red hair.

"You can't just keep winning, Lissa," she said, angry now. "I took *special trouble* to make sure this time. I sent you over that railing so you couldn't ever mess up my plans ever again. *You aren't supposed to be alive.* You aren't playing fair—you've tricked me."

She started toward me, her fists balled up. "You tricked me again."

Then the cop moved fast and grabbed her arms and pulled them behind her and slapped handcuffs on her, all the while telling her her rights. But she wasn't listening; she just stared at me, her eyes wild, until they took her away.

That must have cleared up a lot of things that I don't understand, because after that the cops pretty much left us alone.

I was glad to see Mama; I think it had been a long time since I'd seen her. She looked older than I remember. For some reason there's this memory I hadn't thought of in years that keeps coming back to me: how, when I was little, if I was sick or woke up crying from a nightmare, she used to rock me in the hallway in Gran's old wooden chair with the needlepoint seat. And as she rocked back and forth, that old wooden chair would squeak and creak until after a while, it sounded like it was singing to the rhythm. There was a long mirror hung on a door at the other end of the hall, and in the dim glow of the night-light I could look at our reflection framed in that mirror as though it was a special photograph of just us two, lost in time, and I felt so safe.

When we were alone in the hospital, she talked some about Papa, and how I was the apple of his eye and all. She said that, after all this time, she still misses him lying next to her in the bed nights, snoring like a bear. I laughed, and then I found myself crying for him like I wouldn't let myself do so long ago—like all the walls between us were finally torn down. Time *is* a funny thing, like Mama said.

Even though I don't have any trouble recognizing Gabe and Mama, the accident affected some of my memory. I can't remember much about life the few years before the accident, much less anything about the accident itself. The doctors tell me that happens sometimes. I might remember someday, and I might not.

When they brought me home from the hospital and Mama left us alone, I didn't even recognize my own kids. Gabe had to introduce us. Bug came right up to me and hugged my legs and said, "Mama, you *home*, Mama." But Hailey hung back, like she didn't much know me either, especially when I tried to hug her.

Gabe told me, "Give her time." And I will. When I see how smart they are, it's hard to believe they're mine.

They tell me I had two best friends. I don't know why I didn't remember Becka, the one who apparently tried to kill me, but I remember Cindy. Anyway, Cindy don't come around much anymore. When I asked her on the phone why not, she finally broke down and told me I ain't the same person since the accident, and that I'm changed from the old Lissa she knew. I asked her how I'm changed, but she says it's too complicated a thing to explain. Of course I acted hurt, but the truth is, from the few things I'm starting to remember about the old Lissa, it seems like an improvement.

And Gabe? Sometimes I catch him looking at me at the oddest moments, like this morning in the kitchen, when I was just standing there making our sandwiches for the picnic, or when I was outside playing with the kids. It's like, in some ways, he's seeing me for the first time, so I know he must see a change in me, too. I had to ask him if I was different in a good way or a bad way, and he thought for a moment. Then he said, "I think we're *both* changed, and it's going to be up to each of us to make it a good one."

"Then we'll do it together," I told him.

One night after I got Bug and Hailey off to bed, I fixed Gabe and me a snack of crackers and Cheese Whiz from the kitchen and took it into the living room on a little plate. Gabe had the radio on and it was playing something pretty and soft. I was standing in front of him with the plate when he swept me into his lap and started moving the chair around like we were slow dancing. We forgot about them crackers after that.

I don't remember Sera at all. When I ask Gabe about her he looks sad, and says she's somebody nice we met who just wanted to take care of us for awhile. I tell him I don't understand about her, or why she had to die like that. I guess we'll never know.

Last night I had an idea. I said, "Gabe, you know them little carvings you do?" When he said yes, I said, "Well, why don't you make up a whole mess of them and we'll take them over to that little shop down at the waterfront?"

From the table I picked up a seagull Gabe carved from wood, its wings spread out in flight. "This is good," I told him. "I don't know why I never noticed before."

He turned red and said, "They aren't that good,"

"They *are*, Gabe," I said. I held it up to the light. "*I'd* buy one."

He smiled and said, "In that case, I guess I'd better try it."

All Gabe needs is a little faith in himself and somebody to push him a little, and I believe he could do just about anything he set his mind to. Maybe even walk again someday.

Now, looking over at him as he watches the kids, I study the kind lines of his face, the way his hair blows in the salty breeze coming off the water, the strong muscles in his arms and hands that get him around in the chair, and I realize for maybe the first time what a good man he is. I tell him so, and he looks at me like I remember he used to a long time ago.

"I love you, Lissa," he says. "I always have."

All of a sudden Bug and Hailey are walking toward us, carrying the kite that's still flapping in the wind, with strange grins on their faces. Then out from behind them limps a little dog. It sits down on the sand a little ways away from us, its ears perked up and its little, black-masked head tilted.

"It only gots free wegs, Mama," Bug says. "But it wets me pat him."

Hailey has stopped next to Gabe, but now she steps up to me, too. "He's been hurt, Mama," she says, and Gabe and I can see an ugly, black scar running down its nose. It looks fresh.

"Where do you suppose he came from?" I ask Gabe.

He shakes his head. "I never saw him out here before. He's got no collar and his ribs are poking through. Little thing must be lost."

"I wanna keep him," Bug says softly, wiping his nose on his shirt.

Then I notice all three of them looking at me, all with the same expression in their eyes, like I'm supposed to be the one to make some life-changing decision or something. So I do.

I say, "Never mind all that. Come on now, it's getting late. We been out here long enough."

Hailey's small shoulders sag as she slowly picks up the kite, and Bug screws up his face like he's gonna cry.

I smile at them. "Besides," I say, winking at Gabe, "looks like we got us a hungry mouth to feed."

Gabe winks back at me and we all walk home together, Hailey and Bug so excited they're both talking at once, their new friend limping between them. And with his mouth hanging open like that, you could swear that little dog is laughing.

Acknowledgements

I am indebted to so many people who had a hand in the making of this book, whether directly or indirectly.

I would like to say a special thanks to my **editor, Marg Gilks,** who not only guided me with her insight and skill, but also gave me so much needed encouragement throughout.

Also, a special thanks to the wonderful people at **Xlibris**.

I am deeply grateful to:

Cover artist Scott Williams, a creative genius who also happens to be my nephew,

Photographer Jeni Walden for her patience and expertise with the author photo,

Mindy Barker for her title page art (but most of all for being the most wonderful daughter *ever* in so many ways, and for blessing me with a bright and awesome grandson, Nicolas),

My amazing parents, Roy and Jane Marshall, for their invaluable ideas, enthusiasm, and encouragement, but most of all for loving me—no, *all* of us—unconditionally,

My beloved big sister, Kathy Jewell, for allowing me to tag along and admire her all those years ago, for saving me from the termites (and Lord only knows what else!), for her friendship and her wonderful humor,

My niece, Jordan Marshall, for inspiring me to do what makes me happy, and for helping me to be more "dimensional,"

My nephew, Tré Yager—the little boy who loved books and gave names to bumblebees and all too soon grew up to be a remarkable young man—for his very existence,

My Uncle Bobby Cochran—even though he is miles away, his artistic brilliance still inspires,

And of course, undying appreciation goes to my love, John Walden, for his patience and support, for loving me for myself, and for the gentle nudge that got me writing again.

Made in the USA
Lexington, KY
04 December 2010